ABIGAIL HOPE KIM

FOR SUCH A TIME AS THIS

First Edition
ISBN: 979-8-9952780-0-9

Cover illustration © 2026 by Abigail Hope Kim
Cover design © 2026 by Abigail Hope Kim
Interior design © 2026 Abigail Hope Kim

This is a work of historical fiction inspired by the biblical story of Queen Esther. Some names, characters, and events have been fictionalized for narrative purposes.

FOR MY PARENTS,
EARTHLY AND HEAVENLY.

AND FOR YOU, DEAR READER

AEGEAN
SEA
GREECE
ASIA MINOR
SU
EGYPT
NILE
ARABIAN DESERT

HINDUKUSH
BAKHTRIS
INDUS
SA
N
W
E
S

And who knows but that you have come to your royal position for such a time as this?

—Mordecai the Jew, 473 BCE

GILGAL

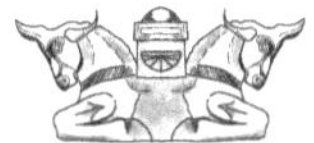

T THE SNAP OF STONE AGAINST STONE**, the flame flickered to life, a languid whisper in the dark. The brisk night air bent the warm glow, threatening to snuff out the light with each violent gust of wind. Mithra hissed as a drop of hot oil rolled onto her hand. A searing pain snaked through her skin. She shook her hand to quell the sting, hoisting a torn cloth bag over her shoulder. Her rattling heart drowned out the roar of the desert gales. Adrenaline electrified her veins. She could almost taste her freedom.

Mithra pulled back the tent cloth, revealing a sliver of Gilgal, the Israelite encampment of tents and fires. She peered through the crack, straining to discern any sounds of life. The guards had fallen asleep against their posts, snores drowned out by the howling winds. She snuck through the opening, pulling her hood lower over her face. Mithra tried to ignore the ache

"

between her legs, a reminder of the death sentence hanging over her head.

The desert gusts pelted her with grains of sand in needles across her face. The air was dry, each breath more painful than the next. Mithra squinted at the night sky through a swirl of sand. *The brightest star would lead her home.* Before a group of Jews had stolen her mother, she had always reassured Mithra that their people never veered from that shining emblem. Her heart flared at the white dot in the sky, the compass to home: Ramoth-esh. The nomadic oasis she had always considered home, even after King Agag purchased her as a slave for pleasure. Ramoth-esh was never in the same place twice, but its name always remained: *heights of fire.* A name worthy of the Amalekites.

But everything had changed. King Agag was dead. She could still smell the blood as she trudged farther away from the campsite. A putrid metallic odor invaded her senses, a grim reminder of her last moments with the king. If she closed her eyes, she could relive every moment—the crazed desperation of Agag's voice, the tears she forced back, the affliction of her body as he subjected her to the final night of his life. She could still conjure the sight of Agag, no longer king, in chains as that bearded Israelite plunged a sword through his heart. *Samuel.* That's what the others had called him.

Agag had been stripped of his crown. Hair and blood matted to his face in gruesome patches. *For Israel!* the Jew had cried. A coldness had overtaken Mithra as she gazed upon the king, helpless in the same way she had been the night before.

Her lips stung as she smacked them together. A trickle of blood crept from the cracked skin, rolling down her chin in a dark stream. Mithra hadn't the faintest idea of how far Ramoth-esh was, but it didn't matter. She had to get away. If any Israelite discovered she could be carrying Agag's child, her grave would stand right beside his. He was clever, she had to admit. A king's legacy was nothing without heirs. Of course, *she* had to suffer for the king's actions while he rested blissfully in death. Leaving Gilgal was an absolute. Even if she never reached Ramoth-esh, she would rather perish at the hand of nature than at the hand of an Israelite.

Step by step across the dense desert carpet, Mithra moved with fire in her heart and a single promise: if she carried Agag's child, that child would restore what her generation could not. Bring redemption from the ruin wrought by the Israelites. She repeated the vow under her breath like a mantra.

Her eyes lifted to the sky, fixed unwaveringly on the brightest star.

Five-hundred years later

HAOS CANNOT EXIST WITHOUT SILENCE. In the absence of silence, chaos lost its meaning as a creature of disorder. Silence must exist for the reality of non-silence. Haman's silence was his mother's comforting presence and her devotion to discipline. It was his mother's voice as she regaled him with tales of the brave King Agag, the valiant Amalekite ruler who perished at the dirty hands of the Israelites. It was a silence he would never enjoy again.

The sun sank low below the horizon, making way for veils of dusk to take over the night. Haman sat on the floor of his family's tent, back hunched as he pored over the lines his father had commanded him to study. Though Haman would have preferred to be sleeping, he learned to stop complaining. His father sternly warned him that a life without knowledge was worthless. And no son of his would ever lead a meaningless life.

He counted off the characters in his head, staring meticulously at each line of text. The back of his eyes burned. Each mark had to be perfect. He had grown accustomed to the weight of the brush under his hand and the smooth gliding of ink. Each stroke left a dark trail in its wake. Haman held the parchment up to his face, admiring his handiwork.

"Imma!" The young boy ran to his mother, her face placid as she wrung water out of a cloth. Haman held up the parchment, the corners of his mouth upturned with an eagerness for approval. "Look at how neat my lines are. Do you think Abba would be proud?"

His mother looked down and smiled faintly. "Your Abba would be proud to have such a scholar for a son." She caressed his cheek lovingly. "But you must be going to sleep now. A great boy like you needs rest to be even greater."

"Where's Abba?"

"Your father will return soon, which means you should be sleeping by the time he comes back. You don't want to displease him."

But rest would not come for a long time.

Haman slid under the covers, closing his eyes. Tomorrow, he would write even neater lines. Maybe he would ask Imma and Abba to tell him another story. Haman rested in the familiar sound of his mother's movements, of the soothing crackle of the bonfires outside, of the creatures of the night singing their familiar songs.

Goats bleated in the distance. Haman shifted in his sleep, irritation quickly rising in his chest. What could be disturbing the town's herd at such an hour? He pressed his hands over his ears, but the bleating only grew louder. And louder.

Haman sat up in the sheets with a groan, rubbing his eyes. "Imma, what is all that noise—"

A blood-curdling scream pierced the night air. Haman jolted upright. A cacophony of shouting followed in a strange language. His Imma threw back the flaps of the tent, eyes widening in terror. A vibrant orange glow cast over her skin. Smoke filled the tent with heavy ash, springing tears into his eyes. *Fire*.

She grabbed Haman by the arm, her grip leaving an ache in his muscles. The fear conquering her dark eyes would haunt him for the rest of his life. "Haman, we must leave. NOW."

It was like stepping out into the full wrath of the gods. Walls of fire surrounded them, flames dancing hellishly on rooftops. Dirt kicked up from the ground as people bolted from the blaze and the strange men. The goats had escaped, their shrieks ringing with panic. Some men charged at the invaders with spears, but their fight was futile. Haman's lungs shriveled at the smoke. He held his breath, but the ferocious pounding of his heart forced the noxious fumes into his body.

"Stay close to me, Haman." His Imma clamped the fabric of her dress over his mouth and nose. Her hand was shaking.

Haman nearly collapsed with relief as his Abba appeared in the distance. His face was smeared with soot. He enveloped them in his arms, urging them forward into the darkness of the desert. Haman felt the fire's heat against his back as Ramoth-esh burned to the ground, the oasis he had known all of his life. Vomit rose to his throat as he nearly tripped over his friends, his neighbors dead on the ground. Spears protruded from their guts, faces bloody and wide with terror.

Haman gripped his Imma's hand, knuckles turning ghostly white. He had never run in terror for his life before. His lungs seared with pain. Without warning, he tripped over a rock, tearing the skin at his knee. Haman lurched backwards as an invader wrestled his Imma out of his grip. Haman screamed. He stumbled forward in a desperate craze. The man thrust his foot into Haman's stomach in a violent kick. He heaved to the side, unable to suppress the bile any longer.

Haman could hear his father shouting and the cracking of bones, but he hardly registered the sounds. His gaze never strayed from his mother as she thrashed against the man, but his grip on her waist was too powerful. He held a spear, the metal edge glinting menacingly. Haman watched as the man lifted his arm. Time stretched and snapped all at once as his Imma pushed Haman into his father's grasp.

"Leave!" she screamed, but her words teetered off into a splutter. The man forced a hand over her mouth, his fingers dirty and thick.

Haman's feet abruptly left the ground as his father swept him into his arms. He shrieked against his Abba's grip, furiously pounding his fists against his back. But the fight was futile. Tears blurred his vision, the salt of his anguish mixing with the lingering taste of vomit. Haman recognized his mother's form as she slumped to the ground, a dark silhouette in the violence. The scene was haunting. Great waves of fire cast a warm glow around her dead body.

Haman yelped at a sudden sharp pain in his right cheek. He pressed a hand against his face. The blood was sticky and black on his palm. He looked up. The man who murdered his Imma, grinning fiercely, had thrown a sharp rock and sliced his skin open. His tears agitated the sting, but he could hardly bring himself to care. *Imma!* he wanted to cry. But no sound came out.

Haman wasn't sure when he went unconscious. He woke up in a tent with his Abba by his side. His head pounded.

He lifted a hand, delicately prodding the bandage against his cheek.

"Abba." His voice was still hoarse from screaming. "Where are we?"

His father looked down at him, eyes lined with dark circles. His shoulders drooped with an invisible heaviness. "Never mind that, Haman. There is an empire nearby that will provide us with safety, but you'll need rest for the journey."

Haman fell back to his side. The realization struck him like an anvil, overwhelming him with his nightmarish reality. *Imma.* A lump rose in his throat, but he forced his sorrow down. A single tear escaped his eye. It rolled down his cheek, staining the ground with a dark circle. His Abba took a deep breath. Haman wondered if he, too, was holding back tears.

"Abba?"

"Yes, Haman?"

Haman turned to his beaten face. "Who were the men that took Imma? They spoke a language I could not understand."

The look in his eyes shifted. Some of the weariness was replaced with something deeper, something more loathful. "Son, do you remember the stories we told you about King Agag?"

"Yes, Abba."

"And do you remember that the Jews, the people of Israel, sought to annihilate our people?"

"Yes." Haman wasn't sure where his Abba was going with this. Why would he bring up stories that happened hundreds of years ago?

"Haman, you must understand that those were not merely stories. The hatred between our people and the Israelites has not lessened over the course of a few centuries." His Abba began playing with the hilt of a dagger, its bronze glinting faintly in the tent's darkness. "Those men who stole your mother were the people of Israel."

Haman said nothing. He turned over with his back to his father. Raising a hand to his cheek, he removed the bandage silently. His finger glided over the valley carved into his skin, over the blood that crusted around the wound.

Rest never came.

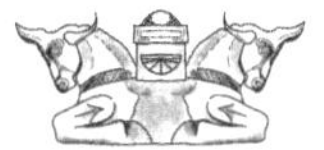

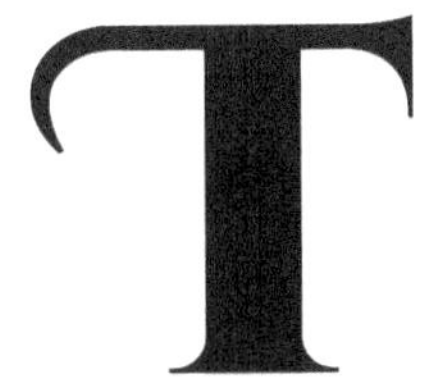HE WINE WAS ENCHANTING. Newly purchased from a wealthy city in the south. Or perhaps the north? Xerxes shook his head. He tilted the warm vessel to his lips once more, shoulders loose with ease. What did it matter? He was the king of Persia, not a lowly merchant.

His eyes glazed across the busy scene before him. No feast under the eyes of the king ever contained a dull piece. Ivory curtains draped from great golden pillars. Guests leaned on columns of marble, wine vessels never straying too far from their grinning teeth. His advisors, the finest nobles in the land, sat on either side of Xerxes, dressed in rainbows of finery as they gorged on delicacies. The king sat contentedly, his mind overcast with clouds of alcohol. He disliked being left in the dark, but this numb fog of pleasure Xerxes always welcomed.

"Would my lord like another drink?" Memucan raised a sleek bottle beside him, words slurring in a drunken stupor.

The king snatched the flask out of his advisor's hands. "How could one refuse?"

He chuckled. "I presume Your Majesty is enjoying the festivities?"

"Quite so," Xerxes grinned broadly. He could feel the reins of alcohol tugging at his brain, gradually assuming power over his thoughts. Not that he minded. After all, the finale of grand celebrations always called for further extravagance.

"It is curious to me how elusive Queen Vashti has been for the past several weeks." Carshena garbled at his right. "Is she so preoccupied with her own affairs to spare even a small visit?"

"Indeed!" Admatha exclaimed boisterously. "Where is that beautiful woman?"

Xerxes took a large swig of drink and paused. Where was his alluring queen? She couldn't have business that mattered more than pleasing her husband. A satisfaction washed over Xerxes as he recalled the fullness of Vashti's lips, the defining curves of her body. There was no woman more arresting than the queen of Persia. The king gazed at the sea of men before him, throngs of officials and high-ranking princes. Surely they should also admire Vashti's beauty. A queen was nothing without winning features.

He turned to the seven eunuchs positioned behind him, addressing the closest guard. "Zethar!"

The hefty soldier peered down at the drunken king, hands folded respectively at his front. "Yes, my lord?"

"See that the queen stands beside me for the rest of the feast." Xerxes grinned in his seat, fumbling his wine vessel. "Round up your guards and place the royal crown upon Vashti's head. I want her radiance displayed before all these men."

"As you wish, Your Majesty."

"Very good, my lord!" roared Carshena as Zethar led a group back into the palace. "It's about time this feast grew interesting."

Noises of agreement resounded over the nobles beside Xerxes, eliciting a broad smile out of the king. Everything was unfolding marvelously. The wine cascading down his throat only heightened his glee.

"Your Majesty?"

Xerxes turned to Zethar. Vashti would finally give him something even more delectable to feast on. "Ah, excellent. The queen is with you?"

"I'm afraid not, my lord."

The world went silent. Xerxes's voice took on a dangerous edge, quiet with building rage. "And why would that be?"

"Her Majesty does not seek to be flaunted," Zethar honed in on a spot on the floor, avoiding the king's gaze. "We attempted to seize her by force, but she did not wish to leave the noble women dining with her. If a matter is urgent, she requests that you come to her privately after the banquet. Our apologies, my lord.”

“Your apologies?” A violent red clouded the king’s vision. His voice was growing louder, frightening and enraged. “Seven men couldn’t overpower one woman?”

“Your Highness, it is against the law—”

“I am the law,” Xerxes boomed. “I am the king of Persia! No one defies my orders, not even the queen.” He could feel eyes boring into the back of his head, tension sparking in the air. Whispers and fear of the king’s wrath had replaced the jubilee in the courtyard.

“What must be done with Queen Vashti?” King Xerxes spat, turning to his advisers. “What punishment does the law yield about a queen who directly defies the king?”

“Your Majesty!” Memucan bellowed. “Not only has Queen Vashti wronged the king, but she has done a great disservice to everyone in your empire! Every wife will hear of what she has done, and they’ll detest their own husbands. How will we put an end to their disrespect?”

Hums of approval chorused across the men, Xerxes among them. If word of Vashti’s disobedience spread, the women of his empire would flare into an unwanted rebellion against their husbands. Wives needed to know their rightful place by serving the men of their households.

"I suggest issuing a decree throughout the empire." Memucan continued. "Sign an irrevocable law by the power of the king. If it pleases Your Highness, sentence Queen Vashti to eternal banishment. Forbid her from ever returning and seek a new queen worthy to replace her. I fear this is the only way to restore order in our homes."

Xerxes nodded in firm agreement, taking a mighty swig of his drink. Yes, he couldn't have the women of his empire incite a rebellion. Queen Vashti was a disease infecting the people with an unacceptable spirit against the king. He would find a new queen. Beauty was easily replaced. Xerxes thrust his goblet to the heavens, bellowing, "Hear me! From this day forth, Queen Vashti is never to show herself before me. I banish her from my empire."

The courtyard rippled with uneasiness. All eyes fell on Xerxes, but he hardly noticed beyond the inebriated haze in his mind.

"Your Majesty," Carshena piped up. Had his voice always sounded that quiet? "What shall we do?"

Xerxes shook his head, wrestling for control over his senses. He slammed his wine goblet onto a nearby tray, overcome with a fresh surge of rage at Queen Vashti. *Former Queen Vashti.* "Let the people know their queen is no more," he began. "And see Vashti out of the palace. Make sure she never returns."

2

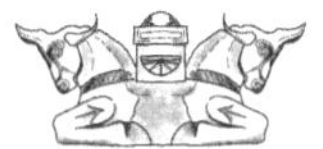

STHER GAZED AT THE BOWL OF WATER BEFORE HER, running a finger mindlessly through the liquid. The water was restless. Ripples trailed along the path of her fingertip, then more followed. It only took the slightest movement to influence every drop in the bowl, the lightest touch to send a wave of impact through the surface. A faint reflection of her face stared back at her, warped in undulating angles at each swell of the water.

"Is there a reason you're staring at yourself so intensely?"

Esther turned, a smile captivating her lips. "Abba." She reached for his wrinkled hand with a gentle squeeze. "You're back early."

The smile lines etched beside his eyes creased as Mordecai enveloped the young girl in his arms, chuckling softly. "I hope my premature return isn't unwelcome."

"I suppose I can tolerate you for a bit longer," laughed Esther. She grabbed a basket of sweet cakes she had slaved away the night before to prepare. The fruits of her labor were gratifying, but the daunting cleaning job she confronted afterward had not been so delightful. Esther was certain some flour still clung to her hair. "How was work?" She pulled a light shawl over her dress. "Have you figured out what to do about that scribe?"

A heavy sigh resounded in the room. "Unfortunately, no. He clearly doesn't know how to do his job, but he thinks he's the greatest at it!" Another sigh. "No one can pound any sense into his head. I'm surprised he hasn't been removed from his position yet."

"Abba," Esther chided, shaking her head. "Try to be patient. I don't blame you for being so upset, though," she whispered as an afterthought, holding back a laugh. "He sounds like a nightmare."

"Regrettably not as temporary as a nightmare," Mordecai chuckled. "But don't worry about me. I'm just comforted knowing my Hadassah is infinitely wiser than I'll ever be."

Hadassah. *Myrtle* in Hebrew. On days when she allowed her mind to stray, Esther wondered when her Jewish name would be uttered by someone other than Mordecai. But her daydreaming was brief. She had lived in Susa long enough to understand that many in King Xerxes's empire had no tolerance for her people. In their perverse hearts, existence was an act of boldness in itself.

Esther shook the thoughts out of her head. Dwelling on the unchangeable was not wise. She was Esther of Susa, and she would remain Esther of Susa.

"I'll be back soon." Grinning broadly, she held up the basket, emanating the aroma of honeyed pastries. "I need to deliver some special treats."

The older man raised an accusing eyebrow. "Is that why I woke up to a stain on my floor this morning?"

"Goodbye, Abba! I'll be back soon."

———

The local bazaar never failed to capture all of Esther's senses. Endlessly bustling with activity, her eyes never focused on a single spot for too long. Stands with billowing shades stood erect on either side, displaying fine necklaces and earthy vegetables. The faint sourness of animal dung invaded Esther's nose as her sandals crunched atop the gravelly road. A man raved about the beauty of his apples, the finest apples in the world! A youthful mother cradled two babies as she examined a kiosk stocked with luxurious jewelry. Ahead, a group of children ran amok with laughter, tumbling to the floor in fits of giggles. Over her shoulder, Esther could hear the bark of an old man, drunkenly raving about the foolishness of King Xerxes. She passed by two Persian nobles lingering under the awning of a woven textile stand. Their robes stood like vibrant fires against the brown tones of the bazaar.

"The Jews are stirring up trouble again?" one man spoke.

"They should be grateful we let them stay," the other sneered.

Esther urged her legs to press on faster. She tugged her hood lower, swiping the back of her hand across her forehead. The Susa sun was never kind, and the summer peaks provoked its rage even further. She adjusted her hold on the twine basket, feeling the corners of her mouth dip slightly. Hopefully, the cakes didn't shrivel into soggy, pathetic little puddles. But before she could inspect the pastries, three small bodies came flying at her legs, fisting the fabric of her skirt in their tiny hands.

"Esther!" Leila squealed. Esther never ceased to be infected by her joy. She had stumbled upon Leila in the marketplace just three years before, drawn by her toothy grin. Once Esther had offered her a small piece of cake, their friendship had been sealed. "What took you so long?" Leila jumped with excitement, her curly hair bouncing up and down. "Have you heard the news?"

"News?" The older girl raised an eyebrow. She knelt before the children, eyes alight with mirth at the familiar round faces. "What news? Did someone win a game? Was it you, Shadi?" She pointed a playful finger at the giggling girl.

"Well, I won the game we just played, but that's not what we're talking about," Shadi grinned.

"We're talking about something from the king!" Leila looked ready to burst, cheeks aflame and shoulders tight with excitement. "There's a new royal prolomation!"

"You mean a *proclamation*, Leila?" Amir, the oldest of the children, corrected. Esther breathed out a laugh.

"Yes, yes, that." The little girl waved a dismissive hand. "It said the king is looking for a new queen! There were a few other things written, but oh, you should just see for yourself. Come on!"

Esther lurched forward as Leila grabbed her hand, tugging her toward the center of the bazaar. *Never underestimate the might of a determined youth.* Esther was careful to avoid the toes of her small-boned companions as she stumbled forward, narrowly ducking a dust cloud from a passing wagon.

What could have transpired? Was Lelia misunderstanding something, or was the king indeed searching for a new queen? And if that were true, then what had happened to Queen Vashti?

Leila came to a grinding halt. She pointed at a wooden post surrounded by swarms of bodies. Frantic whispers and bewildered gazes flittered in the crowd. Leila pushed her way through the throng, directing Esther to the front of the crowd. A scroll framed with an elaborate border was the center of attention, its message penned in elegant curves:

By royal proclamation, subjects of this kingdom are alerted of a recent development under the reign of King Xerxes. Let it be known that Queen Vashti no longer holds the position of Her Majesty. Her defiance has deemed her unsuitable for the king's arm, and she has been banished from this dominion. The Crown will begin selecting young maidens to train for the empty seat. Allow this to reflect your lives. Every man shall be the ruler of his household and shall say whatever he pleases in his native tongue under the wishes of King Xerxes and the gods.

"Wouldn't it be marvelous to be queen?" asked Leila dreamily. "Just imagine all the dancing."

Esther furrowed her brow. She scanned the words a second time. What could have occurred to remove Vashti from her throne? King Xerxes was undoubtedly ill-tempered, but to a degree that would prompt the queen's banishment? Perhaps the decision had been beyond his control. But he was the king. Nothing should have been beyond his control.

"Esther?" Leila gazed up into her eyes. "What if you were the queen? What would you do?"

"Well, you've known me long enough to understand I have an enormous appetite," Esther laughed as she tickled Leila's stomach, eliciting a round of giggles from her. "I'd probably become heavy from all those extravagant feasts. But truthfully, I'm not so sure queens lead happy lives," Esther shook her head. "But enough of this. Would you mind gathering the other children? I have a special gift for everyone."

As Esther watched her cakes disappear into eager mouths, she turned the words of the proclamation over in her head. How long would the people of Persia have to wait before order was restored?

3

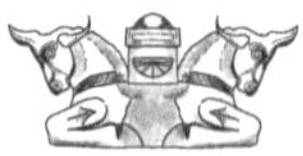

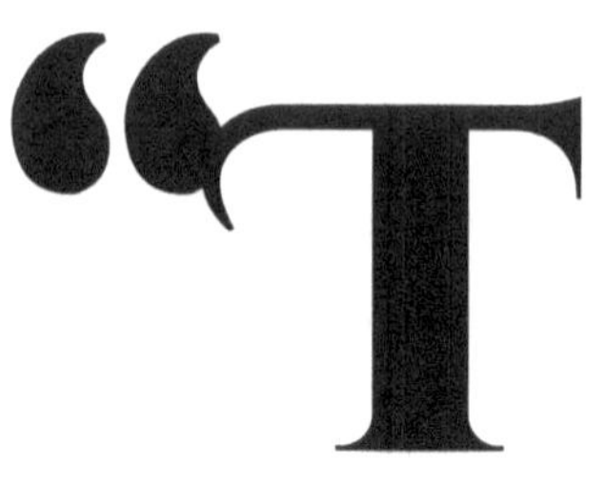**HE KING IS SEARCHING FOR A NEW QUEEN?"** Esther nodded enthusiastically. "It sounds unreal, doesn't it? If I hadn't seen the proclamation earlier, I wouldn't have believed it myself."

Mordecai sighed, raising his bowl of soup to his lips. He shook his head in that amusing manner Esther associated with his disapproval. "This is the problem with King Xerxes," the older man began. "He is quick to make decisions with his mouth rather than his mind." He pointed at his bowl of soup applaudingly. "This is delicious, by the way."

"You are blessed to have an excellent cook in this house, aren't you?"

"Of course, my dear Hadassah." Mordecai rolled his eyes, drawing a snort out of the girl beside him. It was impossible to take his irritation seriously with his benign mannerisms.

Esther smiled, but it soon faded as her heart sobered. The words of the proclamation had glared in her mind ever since Leila guided her to that formidable post. With no queen on the throne, the kingdom was plucking young maidens out of their lives to fill the empty seat. As she watched Mordecai heartily drink her soup, an ache bloomed in her chest for the maiden who would replace Queen Vashti. She would be stolen from her family, forced into a world of conniving politics and loneliness. Trading identity for riches was a price too steep to pay.

Esther could never imagine leaving Mordecai. He wasn't her real Abba—her father had perished in warfare against the Amalekites, the long-standing enemy of Israel. Her mother had passed shortly after giving birth to her. Mordecai was diligent in recounting the sacrifices her parents made to keep her alive, and he spoke of them with great affection. Esther owed her blood-bought existence to them, but it was difficult to be grateful for people she had never truly known. Mordecai was a distant older relative, though he spared no effort in regarding Esther as one of his own. It was Mordecai who taught her that family was more precious than any royal title, that love shone brighter than the purest diamond, and that tradition was the oyster of identity.

"Abba, I'm going to prepare for our Shabbat feast tomorrow." Esther planted a kiss on his cheek before reaching for the vegetables she had gathered the previous day. "An old man like you should be resting soon."

"Who are you calling old?"

———

The world had taken on a warmer tint, a sure sign of the setting sun. Esther splashed her face with water, reveling in the refreshing chill. She slid into her linen tunic designated for Shabbat, an off-white piece cinched slightly by a brown belt. She placed a muted blue shawl over her shoulders. A neat braid fell down her back in tight plaits.

Mordecai stood by the table as Esther began distributing plates of vegetables and flatbread and dates. The familiar aromas sent tingles through her body. As she lit the oil lamps, Esther closed her eyes, the subtle scent curling around her senses with each deep breath. She sat beside Mordecai, speaking their weekly blessings into the air.

Mordecai lifted his glass, beginning his retelling of their ancestors. Esther anticipated this time of Shabbat every week, a time to rest from the week's affairs. He recounted their history with the Amalekites and the evil reign of King Agag, who waged war against the Jews in unprecedented violence. He divulged Israel's noble mission of purging the Amalekites' evil from the world. Though the Israelite King Saul failed to execute Agag fully, Mordecai spoke of the bravery of the prophet Samuel, the true victor and redeemer of their people.

"If there is anything to learn about the Jews," Mordecai continued, "it is that we make many mistakes, but we persevere even when the universe seeks to destroy us. Our people have fought the good fight since the birth of our nation. We must strive to do the same, Hadassah."

As the night of stories and laughter stretched on, an overwhelming joy arose in Esther's spirits. The greatest fulfillment in life was right before her, with her Abba by her side and the lamps flickering low and blessings even more abundant than the jubilee spilling forth from their lips.

———

The small living space Esther and Mordecai occupied was nothing special. Branch-like cracks skirted along the walls, and unwelcome critters often took residence alongside them. Still, Esther adored one small detail of the house: the open window beside her bed. Every night, it blessed her eyes with a perfect view of the stars—a tapestry of nature, a reminder of the infinite wonder that dwelled in her midst.

As much as Esther enjoyed inventing stories of mystical foreign worlds, she adored crafting tales about what she could see. Turning the ordinary into the extraordinary. The mundane into the exciting. The trees into nymphs and dryads. The sun into a blazing protector of humanity. And now, the stars into a map of every single person on the earth. Each twinkling light represented a life, someone fearfully and wonderfully created.

Esther smiled to herself. The world's enchantment hinged on the openness of one's heart. And hers was gaping open. She closed her eyes and drifted into unconsciousness, resting in the sounds of Mordecai's faint snoring and the crickets' melodies.

Esther stood before an endless desert landscape, the sun battering down on her shoulders and the winds drifting aimlessly. She was barefoot, the heat of the sand burning her feet. There was nothing in sight other than endless swaths of dunes and the sky's ocean of blue.

Esther smacked her lips. Her mouth felt as parched as the desert. She swallowed, but her thirst only grew. Esther's eyes widened. Her hands flew to her neck, the dryness spreading down her throat at alarming speeds. She couldn't breathe. An invisible hand was squeezing all the air from her lungs, wrenching all the moisture from her body. Esther fell to her knees, fisting the sand desperately. Water. She needed water. Her mouth gaped open in a silent gasp. As soon as she felt on the brink of death, that she couldn't go another second without breath, the dryness disappeared. Her skin cooled as the sand became a lush green carpet. A faint jasmine hung in the air.

Esther looked up, frozen with wonder. The desert had transformed into a paradise. Cypress sprang up from dead bushes, its full leaves like fire rising from the ground. Myrtle flowers covered the grass as abundantly as sand had covered the desert. Beautiful shades of white peppered the landscape as far as the eye could see. Esther marveled at the sturdy trees, their branches spread open like a welcoming embrace. Pomegranates dangled from the boughs in full bundles, begging to be picked. She reached for one, cracking it open and plopping a seed in her mouth. Her eyes widened with delight. The sweetness traversed all corners of her mouth, sending waves of contentment through her body. Esther gazed at the delectable riches in disbelief. She hastily shoveled a handful of seeds into her palm, opening her mouth to savor the juice once more—

THUD. THUD. THUD.

"Open this door in the name of King Xerxes!"

Esther jolted out of bed. She scanned her surroundings frantically for the myrtles and pomegranates before snapping back to consciousness. Her disappointment was immeasurable at realizing the illusion of her paradise—she could almost taste remnants of the seeds on her tongue. What a blissful dream.

THUD. The fists pounded against the door even more furiously. *THUD. THUD.* What business could someone have at this hour? Esther rubbed the sleep from her eyes. Mordecai was already at the door, his nightclothes wrinkled and hair unkempt with sleep. A trio of men in blood red robes scowled down at the older man, spears glinting menacingly in the moonlight. *Military officials.* "What is the meaning of this?" Mordecai demanded.

One man leered at Esther with rapacious eyes, sending a chill down her spine. Her heart leapt with fear.

"By royal command, you are required to stay at the House of Women before presenting yourself to King Xerxes." The guards lunged for Esther, their rough hands disregarding all propriety. She felt the muscles in her shoulders strain as they wrenched her hands behind her back. Her heart pounded violently, threatening to burst out of her chest.

No. This wasn't real. This wasn't supposed to be happening to her. It was just another dream.

"Hadassah!"

"Abba!" she cried desperately. A soldier forced her head down. She threw herself against him, fighting for one last glimpse of Mordecai.

She caught his gaze for only a moment, a storm of anguish brewing in his eyes. Esther could sense his urgency to run after her, but there was no mistaking the guard's words. *By royal command.* His mouth was moving. He was trying to tell her something, something important, but she could barely hear over the guards' clamor as they tugged her away.

Agony tore through her chest like a dagger. Every instinct in her screamed out for Mordecai. Her pulse thrashed against her neck. She could barely comprehend her thoughts as they surged by the hundreds. This must have concerned the proclamation. She was being selected to compete for the throne. But the king would never take an Israelite for a wife. Her people were foreigners, guests in an empire that barely accepted them. This had to be a mistake. The back of her eyes stung with tears. Fear consumed her in a wave. She forced deep breaths, feeling the cold air slice through her lungs. Esther tried to ignore the rising lump in her throat as she swallowed her tears back.

The midnight chill nipped at her face. She was forced forward, only this time, she didn't fight back. Esther wanted to hurl as the guards' calloused hands gripped and tugged at her bare arms, but she held her head high as if being escorted rather than captured. She raised her eyes to the midnight sky, the same canvas of stars she had gazed at from the comfort of her bed only moments ago. She wanted to return to that paradise in her dreams, to the safety of her bed. Her eyelids closed in a slow swoop, her lashes like feathers against her cheekbones.

Esther's resolve hardened with grit. As fearful as she was, she could not allow herself to be overcome by emotion. She could not alter the lot that had been cast to her. And she certainly could not overpower these guards. She could, however, cling to the wisdom that Mordecai bestowed upon her. Wherever these men were taking her, whatever they would reduce her to, they could never take her wisdom. *All things can become wonderful in their own good time,* Mordecai would say. *All things are worked for the good of those who desire good.*

All things.

4

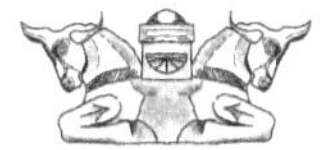

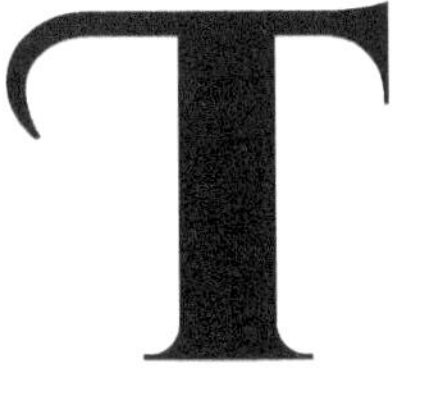HE MORNING SUN WAS VIOLENTLY BRIGHT, the sky the twin brother of blood. Haman gazed out at the bustling city of Susa from his bedchamber window. This was his daily ritual, a chance to look down upon the common man. The streets teemed with women and children hoping to beat the afternoon rush of the bazaar. Camels loaded with mountains of cargo trudged alongside their owners, kicking up clouds of dust with each step. A group of Jewish rabbis communed under the shade of a nearby building, head coverings blocking the stares from passersby.

Haman's upper lip curled in distaste. He turned away from the sight, throwing a sumptuous blue robe over his clothes. The quiet padding of footsteps whispered behind him. A pair of slender arms snaked over his shoulders.

"Where are you going at this hour, my love?" Zeresh breathed, lips hovering beside his ear. Her icy fingers played with the hem of his garments.

Haman swiveled around, meeting his wife's midnight eyes. "I have some urgent business to attend to." They exchanged a knowing glance before he pressed a kiss to her hand. "I shall return soon."

Haman shielded his eyes from the sun as he stepped out into the day, making his way to his partner's meeting place—the alley to the far right of Susa's city square, where most vendors discarded their waste from the marketplace. It reeked of rotting fruit and rusted copper, a place that never held company for too long. A place perfect for Haman's business.

He pulled his hood over his head, slipping into the shadows of the alley. Forcing small breaths through his mouth, he hastily made his way to the back end of the space. His partner already stood in the darkness, a graying beard peeking out underneath his black hood.

Haman dipped his head in greeting. "Do you have what I asked for?"

The man nodded. He pulled out two rolled pieces of parchment held together by a string and a wax seal, an uncanny resemblance to the king's symbol. A side profile of King Xerxes, wielding the royal scepter atop the wings of the gods—the ultimate display of divine authority. "Now, do you have what I demanded of you?" he asked.

Haman placed the scrolls carefully into his bag, rearranging his work materials to conceal the false emblem. He extracted the fifty gold pieces from the pocket of his robes. Delightful clinks sounded as Haman dropped the chunks into the man's hands.

"Trust me, my friend." The edges of Haman's mouth curled upward. "Your riches shall increase tenfold soon."

His partner chuckled, a low sound. "Then I trust your mission will be completed swiftly."

"Indeed." The men bowed. Haman stepped out of the shadows of the alley, removing the hood from his head as he approached a familiar set of Ionic columns and friezes. The grand architecture was topped with a golden finish, a sight worthy of the gods. As Haman walked past the column by the entrance, he felt a slight tug on his robes. An old man sat on the ground with knees tucked into his chest, his gray beard slovenly from neglect. Dirtied robes hung over his skeleton form. Haman kicked his blackened fingers off. A wave of disgust washed over him. Fifteen years of serving in the king's highest courtroom, and King Xerxes still had not purged the Jewish rats lingering by its walls.

"Please, sir," the old man croaked. "Can you spare anything for a humble servant?"

"I have nothing for you, Jew."

Haman spat at his feet. He walked through the open doors of the courtroom, running his fingers along the bronze hilt that never left his bag. The blade had been tarnished by time, though the lion's head etched into the metal snarled as fiercely as it had centuries ago. In its time, the blade had tasted the sweet poison of Jewish blood.

"Never forget." His father spoke with the edge of fifty swords. "They slaughtered our king and destroyed our family, but the name of Agag shall rise again."

He handed the dagger to a young Haman, fingers calloused from hours of studying. As he turned the blade over in his hand, he could feel the weight of his ancestors, of his dead Imma. It was heavy with their blood, their souls, their hatred. His father laid a hand on his shoulder.

"You are part of a long line of brave warriors, Haman. Men who fought for each other and for the gods to eliminate tainted bloodlines. One day, you will help restore our people to greatness, and you will avenge what the Israelites did to our people, to your Imma. You must do what I could not, my son."

Haman brought his hand back to his side, assuming the highest seat in the room.

"My lord," his apprentice spoke. "You seem restless. What is troubling you?"

Haman felt the weight of the dagger, felt the legacy of his ancestors and the weight of his mother's death. He imagined the oblong shape of the two parchment scrolls at the bottom of his bag. He imagined handing them to his accomplices for access to the king's chambers. He considered how heavy a crown would feel on his head, how large the royal signet ring would look on his finger.

Haman smiled. "You mistake my joy for sorrow, my friend. I have never been in brighter spirits."

5

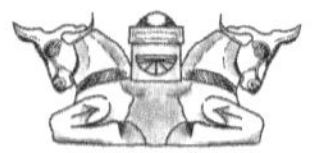

THE AFFLICTIONS OF YOUTH OFTEN FORETOLD THE STRUGGLES OF ADULTHOOD. Esther's memories of that night were vivid, the night Mordecai had not returned home. She had sat by the door against the wall, her anxiety swelling with every passing hour. Her mind leapt to the worst conclusions—that he wasn't returning, that she would be orphaned again. She remembered fighting to remain awake, a battle she eventually lost. She woke to a shake of her shoulders. Mordecai knelt before her with a flurry of apologies, explaining that his work had kept him at the palace overnight. Esther hardly listened. He had returned, and that was all that mattered.

But the tides had turned. Now, Esther was the one who wouldn't return, and the loneliness gripping her heart was far more excruciating. As a child, the hope of his eventual return had eased her panic. But this time, there was no such promise. She could only pray that whatever business the king required of her would pass swiftly, that this too would fade into memory.

They soon left the city square, taking a back route Esther had never seen before. A grand L-shaped building drew closer across the distance. The front doors rose and fell in ornate motifs, impressive carvings of the king surrounded by roaring lions. Golden accents glinted dully along the edges, the severity of the sculptures enhanced by the midnight shadows. The guards handed Esther to a fortress-like man at the entrance. His dark skin blended into the night sky. The nearby light of a torch cast a warm glow over the edges of his face, creating a halo of light around his shaven head. He coldly scrutinized Esther's face. She shivered, feeling naked in her vulnerability.

"She's the last one," one guard spoke. Last one? How many others were there? Anger whirled through Esther's stomach as she recognized the soldier who had leered at her.

The large man nodded, dismissing the two men. He pounded his fist against the door. The wood yawned open to a hallway of blindingly polished marble. Esther was instantly hit by the tantalizing aroma of myrrh oil. The space teemed with girls as they crowded at the sides of the room. Some sat quietly to themselves, fear etched between their brows. Others whispered and giggled, eyeing the surrounding maidens. The man hastily walked up the stairs, leaving her in the sea of strangers. He clapped his hands together, commanding all eyes toward the sound.

"You have been chosen from across the provinces of King Xerxes's dominion," he announced, his voice calm but resonant beneath the domed ceiling. His tone certainly matched his intimidating stature. "Our Great King is searching for a noble, obedient maiden to replace the former Queen Vashti. From this day forth, you will live in this House of Women, and you will be prepared to present yourself before His Majesty when the time arrives."

A faint murmur rippled among the girls, quickly hushed.

From this day forth? As in, forever? Esther clasped her hands together anxiously.

"The servants of the court will tend to you. Ask for anything, and it shall be provided," he continued. "In return, you will obey the laws and words of the king. When your appointed time comes, you will be summoned to the king's chamber to spend the night. He shall choose the maiden who pleases him most, and she shall be his royal bride." Excited whispers pulsed through the room, calming only when the man gestured for silence. He motioned to the eunuchs beside him before returning to the maidens. "We will now escort you to your sleeping quarters."

Esther was rounded off with a group of girls as he led them to the west wing. Her mind was a storm, everything hazy and utterly chaotic. She could hardly acknowledge the beautiful paintings on the walls surrounding her. The girls beside her murmured unceasingly to each other, but their hushed tones faded into the background of her thoughts. Her suspicions had been confirmed. Esther was part of the king's selected group of maidens, and that meant possibly remaining here for months, even years. This had to be some twisted nightmare. Tomorrow morning, she would wake up to Mordecai's snores in their small home, just as she always did. She would prepare breakfast for the two of them, just as she always did. She would venture into the marketplace to purchase food and wash all the vegetables, just as she always did. She would wait for him to return home from the day's affairs, just as she always did.

Esther barely realized she was the only girl remaining until the man opened the last door of the hallway, clearing his throat.

"What is your name, young lady?" His gravelly voice resounded deeply in Esther's chest.

She suddenly remembered a promise she made to Mordecai years ago when they had decided to remain in King Xerxes's empire. The Israelites were foreign guests in a foreign land. Mordecai had gone to great lengths to ensure Esther never strayed from this belief. Her birth name was Hadassah after the white myrtle. Mordecai loved that name—he had chosen it for her, after all. But as long as she lived under the dominion of the Persians, she would be known only as Esther. It was for her safety, he said. So that she could live as normal a life as possible.

"My name is Esther. And what do they call you?"

The look in his eyes was indecipherable. "You may call me Hegai."

Esther bowed politely. "A pleasure. Thank you for escorting me."

"I am only doing my job. I shall see you tomorrow, Esther."

Hegai turned away. Esther stepped into her room, instantly swept by its grandeur. It was infinitely more glamorous and spacious than her home with Mordecai. An inviting bed sat in the corner of the room, fluffy pillows and deep blue silk adorning the mattress. A vanity leaned against the wall, its surface strewn with lavish stores of makeup and a pristine mirror. An opening led to a washroom at the side of the room. The sizable water basin was calling her name after the day's chaos—her body felt tainted by the grip of the guards.

After a hasty bath, Esther sat at the edge of the bed, exhaustion pulling her eyelids down. Her muscles felt like they were melting in the silken sheets. She fell into the arms of sleep, letting rest overcome her senses as she desperately hoped to return to normalcy, to the world she was supposed to be in.

———

"Good morning, my lady."

Esther rose, summoned out of her sleep. She blinked aggressively, raising an arm to shield her eyes from the sunlight streaming through the windows. She almost called out Mordecai's name, but she stopped herself. Everything from the previous night crashed down on her shoulders. The nightmare of being stolen away from her only family was not the mirage she had desperately hoped it to be. That ache in her chest was returning. She quickly stomped it down. If the House of Women was to be her house for some time, she couldn't afford to dwell on the injustice of her situation.

"Good morning." Esther rubbed the sleep from her eyes. A girl stood by the mattress in a simple gown, the waist cinched by a thin silver band. Dark waves of hair framed a youthful face of ivory skin and high cheekbones.

"I'm here to prepare you for the day and escort you to the courtyard." Her voice was gentle. "Come with me."

After learning her name was Adara—quite a pretty name—Esther followed her to the washroom and sat before the large vanity mirror. Adara dipped a towel into a basin of water, brushing the cloth against Esther's skin. Her face had never been attended to with such care. Adara plucked tools from the plethora of beauty products by the mirror, none of which Esther had the faintest idea how to use. Adara began her work, brushing pigment along Esther's eyes and lips and cheeks. The feeling of a brush across her face was foreign to her. It was almost soothing.

"You have such lovely features," said Adara, peering into the mirror beside Esther. The latter hardly recognized herself—the kohl made her eyes longer, more Persian. Her lips looked fuller. Perhaps it was a good thing that she looked less Jewish.

"Your artistry is what's truly praiseworthy," replied Esther, marveling at her reflection.

Growing up in the Persian Empire, Esther had heard magnificent rumors surrounding the gardens of King Xerxes. It was said to reflect paradise itself, with pure water running freely among beds of flowers and trees trimmed to geometric perfection. Nothing could have prepared her for the genuine article. A grand fountain sprang up from the center of a narrow rectangular pool surrounded by heaps of flowers on all sides. The water glistened with clarity, and the blossoms burned with color. Meticulously carved bushes outlined the stone walkways. A long table stood at the center of the garden, holding plates teetering with more food than Esther had ever seen. Fluffy pastries and succulent fruit lay temptingly on silver platters. Heaps of pork glistened under the morning sun. The other maidens had already begun their morning meal, some communing on the grass and others sitting underneath shady trees alone.

Esther took a deep breath. Perhaps she should enjoy this lavish lifestyle while she could. If only Mordecai could see her now, could take part in this feast with her. Her plate became a beautiful artwork, a platter full of color. She steered clear of the meat, lest she taint herself by violating Jewish laws. She may have been Esther on the surface with her painted eyes and lips, but she was still Hadassah. And Hadassah would not stray from her heritage, no matter how foreign the surroundings were.

Esther sat alone under the shade of a lush oak tree, isolated from the other maidens. Their laughter and chatter rang faintly in her ears. She brushed her hands over the myrtles blossoming in neighboring bushes, their white petals greeting her with open arms.

"They're lovely, aren't they?"

Esther looked up. Hegai had approached without a sound, hands clasped behind his back.

She smiled softly. "Indeed. I once had a dream about a paradise full of myrtles."

Hegai hummed. "The other maidens here tell me women prefer roses."

"They're certainly pleasing to behold," said Esther. "But it's unfortunate how quickly roses wilt away. Myrtles endure far longer, and I've heard they release the sweetest fragrance when crushed. Their beauty remains even in destruction."

Hegai nodded, walking away without another word.

———

There was nothing Esther feared more than loneliness. Since her parents' fateful departure from the world, dreadful nightmares had plagued her. Nightmares of Mordecai dying in her arms, his lifeless body growing colder and colder as she sank deeper into a pit of darkness. Haunting visions of corpses as her only companions. On those nights, she was shocked to consciousness in a cold sweat, her heart thrashing violently.

The House of Women seemed like a place where loneliness thrived. She hadn't dwelled in the harem for long, but she had seen enough to feel the sadness in the air. Women sat alone on plush couches, their fine jewelry contrasting the hopeless droop of their shoulders. She had overheard stories in the marketplace of maidens abandoned in the harem after the king enjoyed one night with her, never to be summoned again.

Esther wouldn't be surprised if that were the harem's source of sorrow. She wondered if that was her fate, to be discarded at the end of this charade. Her fear of loneliness was only aggravated; Esther had never felt more out of place amid the jewels and gold and sheer dresses. Every maiden seemed confident in how they ornamented themselves, how they spoke, how they connected with others. How was Esther to live in a land of bejeweled strangers? And could she keep her identity a secret? She surmised she was the only Israelite in the harem. Would she be able to observe her traditions, or was betraying her culture inevitable?

She inhaled deeply. The thick, flowery scent in the air invaded her senses. After relishing in the morning's solitude, Esther had been ushered into a grand bathhouse, the largest in the harem. Steam curled through the chamber, veiling the space in a haze of warmth and fragrance. Rows of copper basins shimmered beneath the lamplight, filled with oils tinted gold and rose. Attendants moved silently between them, their bracelets clinking softly, the air thick with myrrh and sandalwood.

Esther sat stiffly on a marble stool as a servant poured warm oil over her arms, rubbing it into her skin in slow, practiced circles. The scent was intoxicating—rich and musky, almost too heavy to breathe. Her hair was damp with perfume, and her skin gleamed like sunlight caught on glass.

Across from Esther, another girl sighed dramatically.

"If I smell any sweeter, bees will start following me around the courtyard."

Esther glanced up, immediately convinced she had never seen a more beautiful girl in her life. Her skin was darker than tree bark in a rainstorm. The simple robe hanging over her shoulders highlighted the hollows of her collarbone. A large emerald hung from a chain on her neck, complementing her obsidian eyes.

Esther bit back a smile. "Bees make for excellent company."

"Only if you wish for great pain." The girl turned her head, squinting at Esther. "You must be among the king's new selection of maidens."

"How could you tell?"

"You sit like a rod, and you make a show of breathing through your mouth." The girl laughed, a melodic song. "You'll get used to the scent quickly." She flicked a rose petal off her arm, reclining in the seat. "What do they call you?"

"Esther of Susa."

She hummed. "Pretty. I'm Kyra."

Esther smiled. "Are you a part of the king's selection as well?"

A servant passed a clay cup of rosewater into Esther's hands. She took a sip of the cool, faintly bitter liquid. Across from her, Kyra swirled her cup lazily, watching the petals float.

"Of course." She leaned in closer, lowering her voice. "We had little choice. For those of us who have dwelled here for some time, we already serve to please His Majesty, which makes us more viable for the crown." Kyra brought the rosewater to her lips, scrunching her nose slightly. "I can only hope King Xerxes places the crown on my head so I won't be forced to drink this ever again."

Esther laughed. "I'm sure His Majesty will find you most suitable for the throne."

Kyra raised a slender brow. "Do you not wish to be on his arm? You would be wealthy beyond belief."

"My greatest wish is to return home."

Kyra nodded. "I haven't seen my family in years, but you must learn sooner rather than later: nothing exists outside of the House of Women. Once you are here, all that matters is serving King Xerxes. The sooner you forget about your family, the less pain you'll feel."

With a pang, Esther saw that Kyra's face was stone, not a hint of pain or sorrow in her expression. "Surely you miss their company."

"I cannot allow myself to." Her voice took on a different edge, a stark contrast to the playfulness she had exuded just moments before. "But sometimes it is difficult to live this gilded life in solitude."

Esther wondered how much pain she hid behind that statuesque facade. "I believe loneliness is a choice."

"And this place made that choice for me," Kyra replied bitterly.

Esther turned away, sensing a clear end to their conversation. She gazed out at the perpetual rhythm of the attendants—the soft hum of their voices, the trickle of oil into basins, the faint crackle of incense. Esther took in what her life would be until King Xerxes called for her. No Mordecai. No friends. No Leila. No more carefree days in her home or in the marketplace. Just servants and lonely women. Outside, the sun climbed higher and higher in the sky, gilding the vapor that hung in the air as light streamed through the windows.

Kyra had been wrong about one thing. Infinite wonders existed outside of this space of perfume and oils. Kyra had forgotten where she came from, but Esther couldn't do the same. She could not lead her life bereft of purpose, even if she were to remain in the harem.

If she lost her center, then she was better off dead.

6

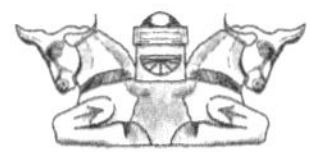

ORNINGS OFTEN ROSE IN SILENCE OVER THE HOUSE OF WOMEN. Sunlight peeked through the lush trees in the garden, painting a shimmering tapestry along the fountain waters. Birds darted in and out of the bushes with chirping melodies. The serenity was nothing like the morning bustle of the city streets.

It was a shame Esther couldn't enjoy it.

"I begin your teaching by revealing the path to success." Hegai's voice filled each corner of the room. Esther's shoulders were tight with nerves.

"There is grace in motion, and wisdom in word. Safety in silence, and power in beauty. Construct your identity around these words. They are your arsenal to success." Hegai walked slowly about the room. His black sleeveless tunic made him a shadow cutting boldly against the morning light. The single golden hoop dangling from his right ear glinted in a white flash.

"Now, I invite you all to peruse the room." Hegai swept his hand in a grand gesture. "There is something amiss in this space. Identify it."

Esther scanned the space. It was an expansive chamber with a comfortable ambience. Meticulous incisions decorated the dark mahogany walls. A table with ornate motifs sat at the center of the room, upholding a golden scepter amid a collection of bejeweled objects. A series of chairs hosting colorful round pillows sat along the edges of the room. She noted the girls beside her, all seated in identical lotus positions atop cushions on the wooden bench. They were all beautiful, though some were startlingly young. Cosmetics aged their appearance, but there was no denying the youth in the fullness of their cheeks, the roundness of their eyes. Kyra sat to her right, an air of slight awkwardness settling between them. Esther cringed. She remembered the bitter note their previous conversation had ended on.

She assessed the space once more. Nothing seemed out of place, but Hegai did not seem inclined to test them frivolously. She had to look where no one else would think to look. Esther squinted at the glyphs on the walls. There was something unique about one etching of King Xerxes. Every depiction of the king was drawn in profile, a style Esther had seen on all of Susa's civil service buildings, even in the harem. But the eastern wall was different. King Xerxes was shown on a fully frontal plane, his eyes staring directly at the viewer. Where had she seen that before? Something seemed familiar to those wide eyes, the curvature of the bodies, the unrealistic proportions. Then it came to her. *Mordecai's manuscripts.* The ancient drawings of their people in his aged parchments. Esther's heart leapt as she squinted harder at the painting. A throng of bearded men who bowed at his feet surrounded the king, some adorned with head coverings. Esther's heart paced even faster. Jews. Those men were Jews bowing at King Xerxes's feet. A shiver crawled through her body.

The room simmered in silence. No other maiden had spoken yet. Esther raised her hand.

Hegai gestured at her. "Esther?"

"A Persian did not paint the artwork on the eastern wall."

She looked for any sign on his expression that she was correct, but Hegai remained emotionless. "Explain," he said.

"All other depictions of the king are traditionally in profile, but this one is not." All eyes had shifted toward her. Esther extended her arm toward the eastern wall, nerves pulsing through her veins. She forced her voice steady. "He is shown frontally, a perspective no Persian artist would ever endeavor to create. And his proportions are skewed, unlike the rigid posture of the other paintings."

Esther felt the burning stares of the other women as her pulse thrashed violently in her neck. What if she was wrong? Just as she convinced herself that she had spoken foolishly, Hegai nodded. "Very good." Esther nearly collapsed in relief. The eunuch turned back to the maidens, continuing as if she had never spoken. "This is the conduct of royalty. You will remain silent unless addressed, but be acutely aware of your surroundings. Things are not always as they seem."

Esther sucked in a sharp breath. Her life at home had been absent from twisted political games and intricate power dynamics. Never had she needed to worry about slouching or the position of her feet and hands or whether she was sucking in her stomach. How could anyone remember all of this information?

Time flew during merry times, and so it did during intense concentration. Esther could not understand why she bothered to pay such careful attention to Hegai's words. If she had no intentions of becoming queen, then why put in such effort? She felt mildly ridiculous as she practiced walking about the room with other maidens. She had never paid such painstaking attention to the lines of her shoulders or the curve of her neck. Surely no one needed to spend this much thought on the simple act of walking. *Then why was she doing it?*

Hegai dismissed the young ladies with a wave of his hand, their whispers and giggles fading into the corridor. Before Esther could follow, his voice cut through the air.

"Stay a moment, Esther."

She turned and bowed politely, signaling her absolute attention.

He studied her for a beat. "Stand upright."

Esther straightened her posture, bringing her hands to her sides.

"Good." Hegai tilted his head. "Bring your chin down. And clasp your hands in front of you."

Heat rose to Esther's cheeks. This was nonsensical. There was no purpose in fixing her mannerisms. Marriage to the king was not an object of her desire. She bit her indignation down, following his instructions. Her body rebelled against the action, so why did her mind refuse disobedience?

"You carry yourself like someone used to being heard."

"Yes, sir. I have a guardian at home who is very attentive to my needs, and I his."

The eunuch's expression was unreadable. Esther had never encountered someone who concealed his emotions so skillfully. She had always considered herself fluent in reading people, but Hegai utterly dismantled her abilities. "It would do you well to remember that His Majesty prefers those who submit to him."

"Is that the kind of woman the king truly notices?"

"I cannot speak on behalf of His Majesty's personal tastes." Something shifted in his countenance as Hegai appraised her. The skill by which he rendered himself unreadable gave Esther the distinct impression that he was a man of deep thought. A man who maintained his insights privately with a kind of solemn wisdom. "I only know that he does not like being challenged," Hegai continued. "Doing so is punishable by death."

Esther hummed. Mordecai often spoke of the king's fragile temper. "You make silence seem like a virtue."

"In the palace, it's considered wisdom."

"Then what do you consider wisdom, sir?"

He paused, then fixed his eyes pointedly at her. "Knowing when to speak, and when not to."

Esther lowered her eyes, thanking him as she swiftly made her way to the door. A flare of embarrassment rose in her chest. She released a breath, forcing her mind to calm. She was not in her home in Susa—she could not speak as freely as she could with Mordecai. Esther had overstepped, even if mildly. *Safety in silence,* Hegai had said. Even if she wanted nothing more than to escape home, to Mordecai, she couldn't make a scene here. Her Abba would want her to succeed in whatever environment she was placed in. It would be dishonorable to relinquish hope.

"Esther, may I ask you a question?"

Esther had been halfway out the door before she paused.

"Anything, sir."

"How did you know the artist was not Persian?" he asked. "Many could have noticed that the piece was not in profile, but you spoke with great confidence as to the artist's identity."

Esther froze. To reveal her assurance that the artist was Jewish was a dangerous path. Yet she could not bring herself to lie to Hegai. Even if she did, something told her he would see right through it.

"I'm simply a lover of the arts."

He gave no indication of satisfaction with the answer. He thanked her, dismissing her with a polite bow.

As Esther lay in bed that night, an epiphany struck her. She was standing at the edge of a dark pit, at the brink of despair and loneliness. Whether she fell or remained standing depended on her strength alone. Would she choose to step forward into that abyss? Escaping the harem was not an option. As strong-willed as she was, Esther could not be so haughty as to believe she could overpower the king's eunuchs. No, she had to remain in this gilded prison. What was asked of her, she would fulfill. Her object was not to become queen, but to make the best of her situation. It was plain that her plan would require submission. Grace would be her compass, not a chore.

Over the next several days of Hegai's instruction, Esther's gaze never left the eunuch as he spoke. She was instructed to extend her right hand in greeting before the noblemen of the court. She extended her right hand. She was taught to bow before the king until her forehead touched the ground. She bowed until the marble kissed her face. She was told to walk as if her feet were floating. She walked with the ease of gliding, keeping her head up as if lifted by an invisible string.

She largely kept to herself, eating meals with only the courtyard flowers for company. The beauty of nature was always a welcome friend, but with each passing sun, Esther's craving for companionship grew stronger and stronger. The free hours of the day were most excruciating—her solitude plagued her the most during those silent times.

Nighttime began to fall over the harem. Sleep typically arrived quickly for Esther, especially after long days of training, but her mind was unusually restless. Thoughts of Mordecai's safety consumed her, even to the most minute detail. Was he eating well? Was he covering the windows to keep the rooms cool? Was Mordecai searching for her? Or had he accepted both of their fates?

Esther kicked off her sheets and walked silently to the courtyard. She lowered herself onto a marble bench. The abundance of bushes and flowers glowed dimly under the covering of night. A torch elevated on an elegant pole illuminated the surrounding space with a soft radiance. She closed her eyes, drinking in the tranquility before the soft padding of footsteps filled her ears.

Hegai took a seat next to her. "You ought to be resting at this hour."

Esther smiled gently, continuing to gaze out at the courtyard. "I wish I could."

Hegai hummed. "It seems I'm not the only one occupied by my thoughts tonight. What troubles you, Esther?"

Her stoic teacher inquiring after her well-being was not something Esther expected. Somehow, it made him more of a human and less of a heartless caretaker. Esther opened her mouth to express that she was perfectly fine, but she paused. Hegai was her instructor, but this wasn't a time of teaching. She didn't need to be perfect in this moment.

"In truth, I'm struggling with isolation." Esther began, dragging her fingers through the flowers beside her. "I miss my guardian at home dearly, and I'm having difficulty connecting with the others."

Silence stretched between them for some time before Hegai spoke. "I understand, Esther. I have guided the women here for years now, and I've learned that service to the king means total sacrifice. People come and go, but I have a love for our crown that triumphs my solitude."

"Is it not impossible to live joyfully while suppressing pain?"

"Dwelling on pain has only worsened my circumstances," said Hegai. "But that makes connections with others so important. I'm certain you will find companionship. Perseverance is an honorable fight, Esther, especially in our relationships."

Silence filled the air once again. It was peaceful, almost sacred, as Esther took in his words.

She smiled, breaking the quiet. "You are a wise man, sir."

"Hegai. Please call me Hegai."

Though his face was barely discernible in the dark, Esther could've sworn she saw a hint of a smile on his face. He rose from the bench, escorting her back to her chambers in the night's quiet.

———

There comes a time when young ladies become more acutely aware of their appearance. For some, it is an instant wariness of the position of their hair, or how certain robes cascaded down the angles of their body. For others, it is a gradual process of becoming acquainted with the concept of beauty, a slow realization of people's perception.

After mulling this over frequently, Esther believed she fell into the latter category. If her mother were still alive, she believed her vanity may have been pampered even more by the presence of another female. Mordecai never concerned himself with external appearances. He valued the condition of one's heart far above vain pursuits. Even so, he unceasingly reminded Esther that she was the most beautiful lady in all the world's empires. She would laugh, jesting about his propensity for delusion as he grayed in years.

Esther wondered if that would change about her, too. With her new fixation on how she carried herself, obsession could also latch onto beauty. She could already feel the harem shaping her, molding her into an indweller of extravagance and vanity. Would she crane her neck to catch glimpses of herself in nearby mirrors or polished goblets? Rise every morning with a compulsion to powder her face and paint her lips?

Esther stepped into the beauty chambers, immediately hit by the warm, woody smell of myrrh. A servant girl escorted her into a smaller room within the chamber. It was a different space, though just as elaborate as the rest of the harem. A vibrant turquoise blue dominated the walls, offset by golden and white floral motifs. Luscious pillows decorated the edges of the room. Tables sat beside the benches, holding bottles of perfume and jars of oil. Esther couldn't imagine the cost of even one perfume vial, let alone a collection.

Esther swapped her dress for a white robe, relishing in the soft cloth against her skin. She settled into the cushions beside Kyra and closed her eyes as Adara lathered her skin with jasmine. The aroma trickled into her brain, urging her muscles to relax and her thoughts to slow.

Kyra sighed. "The gods have a twisted sense of humor."

Esther's lips quirked in a smile. "You seem to share that with them, Kyra."

She snorted. "I'll take that as a compliment."

The room fell into a comfortable hush, broken only by the gentle slosh of oil and the soft scrape of the servants' sandals. Esther sensed Kyra's gaze on her, the scrutiny burning more intensely with each passing second.

"I don't like you," Kyra said plainly.

Esther opened her eyes, turning to Kyra on her side. "Why?"

"Do you know why the gods have a twisted sense of humor?" she began. "They put someone like you in a place like this. Someone who seems to believe this world might be kind, like some kind of Lady Sunshine." She glanced over. "And they expect the rest of us not to resent the joke." Her tone was almost indifferent.

Esther remained silent.

"Do you know what this place does to people?" Kyra continued.

"Yes, I do."

"No," Kyra said. "You *think* you know what it might do. You haven't been here long enough to see what it *will* do."

"You're right," Esther said after a moment. "I haven't."

Kyra blinked, thrown off just enough to look away. A servant pressed warm oil into her shoulders. Esther watched her jaw loosen, the lines between her brows smooth over.

"I think I know what it is about you," Kyra said. "You're far too calm. Calm like that never survives here. It either rots or gets sharpened into something ugly."

Esther watched the jasmine drip from her wrist, tracing a slow path to her elbow. "Then I suppose I'll discover that for myself."

"You say that as if you have a choice."

"We always have a choice."

Kyra turned fully toward her, eyes sharp. "None of us has a choice. Once those gates shut and the perfumes start, they teach you how to smile through the emptiness right away. No one is free."

"You chose to believe you're trapped, Kyra," Esther said firmly. "But you can always choose differently."

The servants stepped back from the girls, exiting the room behind Adara. Kyra leaned forward, elbows on her knees. "Listen, I don't hate you, Esther. I just don't trust you. Girls like you believe they can stay soft. The rest of us—" She shrugged. "We've already paid for that mistake."

The room settled again, the steam curling low around their ankles. Esther shifted, the cushions sighing beneath her. "You said you don't like me. Do you still?"

Kyra hummed in thought, drumming her fingers together. "I don't like what you remind me of," she finally said.

"And what's that?"

"That I used to believe I could walk through this place without it touching me." Kyra stood, tugging the robe tighter around herself. "You'll lose that belief."

"Perhaps," Esther said. "But until I do, I'll need someone honest enough to tell me when I'm being foolish."

Kyra paused at the doorway, turning back. "Are you asking for trust?"

Esther smiled slightly. "I'm asking for truth."

Kyra considered her before giving a short nod. "I can give you truth. But don't mistake that for kindness."

"I won't," Esther said. "And I won't mistake your bluntness for cruelty."

A corner of Kyra's mouth twitched. "Careful, Esther. You'll think me nicer than I actually am."

Esther smiled, feeling the slightest warmth bloom in her chest. "Maybe you think yourself crueler than you actually are."

The edge of her mouth raised, some of the edge removed from her voice. "As you say, Lady Sunshine."

7

THE CHEST OPENED WITH A CLICK. It was beautiful. Golden and turquoise flora embellished the dark wooden casing, giving the edges a slight sheen in the light. Esther's finger glided smoothly over the embossed swirls. A collection of brushes lay neatly assembled in the upper interior, not a single hair out of place. Esther looped her finger through the gilded ring of the bottom drawer. A gentle clinking sounded as she pulled the container open, revealing stacks of darkly pigmented pots.

Esther screwed the lid off the black pigment. She grabbed the thinnest brush, coating the bristles in powder. Tiny clouds of pigment kicked up with each dab. She drew a slender line outward from the end of her eye, mindful of stilling her hand. The tickle of the brush's touch was no longer an unusual sensation. It had almost become strange to go a day without painting her features. Esther mirrored the line on her other eye before assessing her handiwork, turning her head from side to side. A small sense of accomplishment filled her. Though it was not nearly as professional as Adara's handiwork, the liner flattered her upturned eyes. It would have to do. Esther quickly swiped her lips with a dark beige as a knock sounded at the door.

"Come in."

Adara strode in with a procession of ladies trailing behind her. Each maiden donned a spotless white gown, hands clasped in front of their torsos. Their gazes were fixed on the ground, a posture of servitude.

"My lady." Adara bowed alongside the ladies. "Allow me to introduce you to your new attendants, who will be serving you alongside me. We have orders to escort you to your new sleeping quarters."

Esther tilted her head. "Is something wrong?"

"We'll explain everything once you've settled in," said a girl by Adara's shoulder. Her shorter hair and porcelain skin complemented a petite frame, and she spoke with an airy ease. "Please follow us."

Esther's grasp of the harem's landscape had sharpened over the passing weeks. As she fell into step beside the young ladies, she recognized the sweeping hall that opened to the courtyard and the intricate arches framing the beauty chambers.

But as they moved farther, the path bent into an unfamiliar passage tucked behind the bathing rooms. It seemed impossible for the House of Women to grow any more lavish, and still each column rose more imposing than the last, the carved motifs surpassing even the splendor of the halls she had come to know.

"My lady," Adara spoke quietly. "Did you apply your own makeup this morning?"

Esther's cheeks reddened faintly. She let out a gentle laugh. "You've caught me. It's not as easy as you make it appear."

Adara smiled. "I like it."

They stopped by a pair of double doors, framed by a brilliant blue shining with emblems. Adara pushed the doors open, revealing an expanse comparable to the size of Mordecai's home. The ladies entered the room, fanning around Esther as she marveled at the majesty of the space. It was a room fit for royalty. Sunlight poured in through the windows, illuminating the colorful, meticulous designs of the wallpaper. A lavish bed with canopies and golden trimming sat on a carpet spanning across the entire floor. A gilded entryway led to the bathroom, opening to a vanity and a bathing pool with stone steps. It had already been filled with crystal-clear water, flower petals floating delicately along the surface. A clear dome enhanced the room, casting sheaths of light across the space.

And it smelled *heavenly*. Floral and sweet, but not in a sickly sense.

Stunned, Esther stepped back into the bedroom. Had the other maidens also received new rooms? Could it be a test of her humility? Maybe she was expected to deny the opulence. Or was it a reward?

She turned to Adara, the question on the tip of her tongue: *why?*

"We were asked to maintain confidentiality, even from you," Adara spoke, reading Esther's disbelief. A slight smile had taken form on her face. "However, I believe you're capable of filling in the missing gaps."

And then it came to her. Esther knew precisely who had arranged her new situation.

Adara held up her hand. "Before you leave to thank him, allow me to introduce your new attendants."

One by one, the ladies bowed before her and revealed their titles. Seven women in total, including Adara. She searched for distinct features in each to better remember their names. Adara, she was already familiar with. The other girl who had spoken was Elina, glowing from her porcelain complexion. Then there was Nava with her umber skin, Rahi's doe eyes, Amna's sweet countenance, Zarine's rounded nose, and Javaneh's defined brows.

The ladies swiftly drew a bath. The warm water sank deeply into Esther's limbs as she released the week's tension from her nerves. Tingles danced down her skin as her scalp was massaged firmly, and her nails filed to rounded angles. The maidens were careful to avoid smearing the cosmetics she had applied to her face. After emerging from the bath, Adara extracted a brilliant blue dress. The neckline cut across Esther's shoulders in an elegant swoop. It was like a gown of water, hanging marvelously on her frame and cascading in waves down her waist.

As Esther gazed at the jewels in her hair and the priceless fabric of her clothes, guilt tugged at her conscience. While she abounded in luxury, her Abba was in the dark, alone with no way to guarantee her safety. She yearned to tell him she was more than content, that this would all soon pass.

Once they reached the courtyard, her handmaidens bowed and whisked away. Esther inhaled deeply. Nature seemed especially alive today. The sun beamed down on the land, and morning creatures communed in the trees with expressive chitters. The golden rays cast a comfortable glow over her skin. Flowers bloomed to life in the bushes, a wonderful assemblage of color against a green canvas.

Esther advanced toward her target. Hegai stood monitoring the ladies near the edge of the courtyard, his arms crossed and mouth set in its characteristically stern line. She let a comfortable silence stretch between them as she stood next to him, gazing out at the maidens.

"If you're here to thank me, there's no need," Hegai finally spoke.

Esther smiled. She wondered how often anyone thanked him, a man tasked with eternal servanthood. "How did you know I would figure it out?"

"Because it's you."

"You exercise much generosity," said Esther. "Why keep it in the dark?"

"You're mistaken. I'm not a generous man," he replied, gazing at her intently. Though his expression remained unmoving, his eyes communicated a message far deeper than any smile he could plaster on his face. "I simply wish to care for those valuable to me."

Esther bowed, walking away from the eunuch with steady warmth written on her heart. She knew the implications of Hegai's words. The extravagant chambers and servants had not been a trick or a test of humility. It was a favor. An extension of kindness.

Armed with a plate of fruit, Esther lowered herself into the seat beside Kyra, picking up the ends of her dress to avoid sullying the hem.

"How kind of you to grace us with your presence."

"Good morning, Kyra."

Kyra shot her an incredulous look. "And what possessed you to sit next to me?"

Esther disregarded the question, happily biting into a plum. "You look wonderful," she said, noting the elegance of Kyra's white gown and golden headdress.

Kyra continued to stare at her, waiting for Esther to leave. She soon relented with a sigh. "As do you," she said begrudgingly, though her tone had softened.

A smile overtook Esther's lips. A small victory.

The two ate in silence before Kyra nudged her side, lowering her voice to a whisper.

"I'm curious to know whether you're acquainted with Zelah."

Esther frowned. "I don't believe so."

Surprise flashed on Kyra's face, a glint forming in her eyes. "How interesting."

Esther looked at her pointedly. "Do you find entertainment in the spectacles of others?"

"The greatest joy," Kyra grinned. She peered over Esther's shoulder. "There she is, the one by the tree."

Esther turned, locking eyes with a dark-skinned girl. Tight curls cascaded down her slender shoulders, and black kohl outlined her piercing gaze. She looked strangely familiar. Esther stretched her mind, unsatisfied when she drew a blank.

There was something about the rise of her cheekbones, the defiant set of her mouth…

Kyra huffed. "Why would you look at her so obviously?"

"How could I not?" Esther lowered her voice to a whisper. "She looks familiar, but I can't remember where I've seen her."

Kyra raised her eyebrows. "Perhaps you've trained with her here before?"

Esther shook her head. "We've never spoken to each other."

Kyra continued. "Well, she speaks of you in a way that suggests a long-standing resentment. She spreads lofty tales about you, but I suspect they're not true." She smoothed out her dress. "Unless you regularly steal from the bazaar, I don't believe you have the gall to commit such crimes."

She did not want to make enemies during her time here. Esther wracked her brain for any moment where she might have wronged someone named Zelah, but she could think of nothing.

"Do you suppose I should talk to her?" Esther asked. "Perhaps to try smooth things over?"

"I wouldn't recommend it," Kyra said, stabbing a berry with her fork. "I've found that such people are extremely difficult, nearly impossible, to rationalize with. I suggest remaining quiet and continuing to be your painfully optimistic self."

Esther hummed in agreement, though she still felt uneasy. After Hegai reviewed their foreign languages for the day, she decided it was time to put her mind at ease.

"Should someone make an enemy out of the queen," Esther began, "though she may not wish it, what would be the wisest course of action to take?"

"It is not a queen's place to make a poor situation even worse," he said. "Remain quiet and observe, for this will grant you the wisdom to determine what is best for the kingdom. Never forget the safety in silence, Esther."

Safety in silence. If there was any lesson that continued to be thrust upon her, it was to seal her lips unless she was spoken to. And yet, Esther could not shake the fear that silence might one day endanger her more than speech, that there would come a moment when quiet would no longer save her.

———

Esther sat alone in her lavish chambers, gazing out the window. She laid out plates of food on the table in a familiar arrangement, the sights and smells a heavy reminder of home. The sun was sinking lower and lower below the horizon. The last days of the week were approaching.

"Adara." Esther had stopped her friend after the other maidens retired for the evening. "Would you be able to get these items from the kitchen for me?"

They had settled into a weekly routine. Adara now knew that Esther enjoyed private meals alone as the week's end approached, and she faithfully laid out her requested ingredients. She never questioned Esther, which the latter was eternally grateful for.

Esther lit two oil lamps, closing her eyes as she set them on the table. Kneeling on the ground, she recited the blessings she had once uttered beside Mordecai, words that filled her with a profound comfort. In her mind's eye, she saw her Abba sitting in their home, eating the same meal and speaking the same blessing in their home with a slight smile on his lips. Parallel lives, but worlds apart.

It was strange to eat a Shabbat meal in so much silence. She refocused her gaze out the window, reminding herself that Mordecai was alive. Somewhere in Susa was their humble home. She would eat a Shabbat meal with him again. It was only a matter of time.

A rustling sounded by the door. Esther frowned. Her chamber doors had been left slightly ajar. She shut the opening closed and returned to her spot on the floor, allowing the golden glow of the setting sun to illuminate the spread before her and the hope in her heart.

8

HE SUMMONS CAME WITHOUT WARNING. Esther rose from her bed, shielding her eyes from the sun as she rubbed the sleep from her face.

"We must make haste, my lady," said Adara, quickly swapping Esther's sleeping gown for a dress. "Hegai requires your presence immediately."

The chamber she entered was almost suffocating. The ceilings were low, and the walls were adorned with stone. There were no windows, only a single light emitting from a brazier at the center of the room. Smoke clung to the air, coating the back of her throat. She counted ten other maidens standing in the line. Esther searched for Kyra, but the only familiar face was Zelah, posture proudly erect in the middle of the procession. Esther quickly took her place at the end of the line. Hegai stood in a dark corner of the room, gazing out at the maidens. No one spoke. The only sound she could discern was the crackle of the fire. Esther snapped out of her sluggish morning state. The air in the room was heavy, charged with a foreboding tension.

The doors swung open, ushering in an older, broad-shouldered man dressed in deep green robes. Esther recognized the brooch on his cloak, a golden circle emblazoned with the king's scepter. *A palace official.* His face bore the severity of calculation, utterly devoid of warmth. Hegai stepped out of the shadows, facing the line of maidens.

"This is Mardonius, an official of the Great King," Hegai said, gesturing to the man. "You are to listen to everything he says."

"I represent Xerxes, the King of Kings." His voice was low and commanding. Mardonius walked slowly in front of the maidens, appraising each one individually. Esther wondered if he could hear how fast her heart was pounding. "I will ask questions, and you will answer them appropriately," he continued. "Should I dismiss you, you are no longer in contention for the throne."

Esther stole a glance at Hegai. He was watching them intently, giving her a subtle nod of encouragement. Her nerves calmed, heart rate slowing.

A maiden at the far end of the line stepped forward, bowing deeply. "My lord, it is an honor—"

"You're dismissed."

The command echoed through the room. Guards emerged from the shadows and took her by the arms, her protest echoing briefly before the doors closed behind her. Esther's breath began coming in shorter bursts, the sound of the slamming doors reverberating in her mind. The room suddenly felt smaller than it had before, the tension in the space growing thicker and thicker.

Mardonius turned back to them, clapping his hands together. "Now, which of you believes mercy is a weakness?"

Zelah's hand rose at once.

"A kingdom cannot survive with softness," she began, her voice ringing clear. "Mercy weakens authority, and it's dishonoring to the gods to diminish power."

"What if a ruler without compassion invites rebellion into his domain?" The man interjected.

"Revolt is easily suppressed for a powerful ruler," Zelah replied instantly. "Fear garners loyalty, which is far more valuable than fragile compassion."

Esther's thoughts leapt to King Xerxes and his grapple with the Athenian revolt. Xerxes was widely feared for his iron-like reign, and yet he struggled to suppress their rebellion. Did that make him a poor ruler? According to Zelah, he was weak. But Xerxes had extended some semblance of kindness to Esther's people by accepting them into his empire, just as his fathers had. He couldn't be one-dimensionally labeled as a feeble king.

The official nodded at Zelah before his gaze landed on Esther. "You do not believe mercy is a weakness?"

"I believe mercy and fear are needed equally," she said evenly. "Neither should rule alone. It is when these are practiced in isolation that they become weaknesses."

"You fail to answer my question directly," the official said.

"I answered what was asked of me, my lord."

"If you believe it's a king's place to show both mercy and fear, then you are charged to protect these as queen." The brazier flared as the official moved closer. "Would you also lie to protect King Xerxes?"

"I would give my life to protect the king," Esther said carefully. "But I would never trade the truth for a performance."

Esther could feel Zelah's eyes boring into her side as the official finally left her to face the other maidens. Relief crashed over her in a quiet wave. One by one, the maidens were dismissed. One for guile, another for panic, and the rest for an eagerness to please until only three remained, Esther and Zelah among them. The pressure on her shoulders grew heavy. Undoubtedly, she had been tested for wisdom and restraint. Had she spoken wisely? Had she said too much?

As Esther was escorted out of the chamber, she stole one last glance at Hegai. The tightness in her chest loosened when she caught the faintest smile resting on his face.

———

The first oddity of the day was the new room. Adara had awakened Esther at the crack of dawn, accompanying her to a chamber that resembled Hegai's teaching space. The plush cushions and ornate motifs were nearly identical, only the windows let in more sunlight. Two desks faced each other at the center of the room, a parchment and an ink pot already laid out on the surface.

The second oddity was the lack of the other maidens.

"Hegai, where are the others?"

"They are to receive instruction elsewhere," he replied. "I would like to introduce someone to you."

A young lady swept into the room. She could not have been over thirty years, and yet her posture exuded the humble confidence of experience and wisdom. Her dark hair formed a wreath of braids adorned by a simple golden band. Her eyes were warm, and the elegant lines of her lips formed a smile, a picture of refinement.

"Esther, this is Fatemeh, the first of several instructors who will join me in equipping you for the throne," Hegai began, "Fatemeh, this is your new student. You won't have a difficult time with her."

He turned to Esther, dipping his head slightly. "You will also receive teaching from me, just as you have been. The other maidens must never catch word of your circumstances."

Esther smiled, though she questioned why she was receiving separate teaching. Had Hegai perceived she was lacking? Maybe Mardonius's test had revealed some weakness of hers.

The thought stung, but she masked it well. "I won't say a word. Though, if I may," Esther added. "Deceit does not seem becoming of a queen."

His face remained stone-like, though she felt a slight satisfaction at the slight quirk of his mouth, as if he were holding back a smile. "Defying orders does not seem very becoming of a queen, either."

A twinkle shone in Esther's eye as she bowed. "Yes, sir."

Hegai exited the room, leaving the two young ladies alone.

"I have been told that you are highly capable." Fatemeh lowered herself at the table, beckoning Esther to sit before her. "I shall teach quickly, and I expect you to keep up." She picked up the stylus from the clay tablet, dipping it in the decorative ink pot.

A morning had never passed so swiftly. The challenge to match Fatemeh's intelligence gripped Esther's mind as she entered a new world of court semantics.

Language was never accidental. All things under the king's dominion were declared good, and they were addressed as such. Not just an army, but a good army, a *kāra*. A good people. A good land. The only true threat to this goodness was the *drauga,* the Lie of disorder set against the king's rule. To combat this great evil, the gods bestowed the ruler with the highest honor as King of Kings. Esther faintly remembered Mardonius referring to Xerxes by that very title.

"The king's many titles go beyond simple courtesy," Fatemeh continued. "To be King of Kings is what makes up his *farr,* his blessing from the gods." She gazed at Esther intently. "When you approach King Xerxes, you approach the highest order in the universe."

The morning passed, and Esther rejoined the other maidens in the courtyard. Her stomach rumbled at the sight of the plump fruit and freshly washed vegetables.

"Someone's hungry today," Kyra remarked.

Esther gestured at Kyra's plate with a twinkle in her eye. "It must be you. There's more food on your plate than usual." Their laughter fused into one melody in the air.

After Adara lavished her hair with perfume and her skin with myrrh, Esther reunited with Fatemeh. A low table and two couches beckoned at the side of the room. An array of food glistened in a spread of breads and dates, and two goblets of wine stood beside the gleaming silverware. Esther lowered herself onto one of the plush seats. She wondered at the lowness of the table and the position of the couches. It was so unlike the wooden dining board she shared with Mordecai.

"You will appear at many banquets with the king, and eyes will be on your every movement. Etiquette must become second nature to you," Fatemeh began, leaning against the pillows. "It is customary to take meals while reclining on couches, though you may also be formally seated. Be relaxed but composed. After all, banquets showcase the generosity of His Majesty."

Fatemeh lifted one of the wine goblets, an elaborate golden vessel resembling a bull's head. Carved flora trailed down the sides of the cup.

"You are to be seated in order of rank and favor," she continued. "If not at his right hand, you will be placed near the king's closest confidants. Toasts begin with the highest-ranking man and end with the lower ranks." Fatemeh lifted her goblet, her fingers joined at the bottom of the vessel. "You must toast in this way, and blessings for the king's health and prosperity must pass from your lips with the utmost grace."

Esther mirrored Fatemeh's motions. "To the King of Kings," she said, taking a delicate sip of the wine. The fluid cascaded down her throat in a bitter stream.

Fatemeh placed her goblet on the table and lifted a utensil, gesturing for Esther to mirror her motions. "Feast with your right hand alone as a symbol of purity. And don't dishonor the king by eating meekly."

Esther nodded, though dread pooled in her stomach. Mordecai had sworn her to secrecy about her Jewish heritage, and she had kept that promise faithfully. But banqueting would complicate matters. Jewish law forbade her from eating impure meats and other foods that would undoubtedly fill the king's tables. Esther was confident she could honor her heritage even during training. Still, she clung to the fragile hope that she would not be chosen as queen at all. Once she returned home, she would be spared the burden of royal feasts and the dangers they posed to her secrecy. Even so, there was something she needed to make certain of.

"Fatemeh, are we required to eat everything presented at the table?"

Her teacher hummed in thought. "You need not concern yourself. Partaking in the meat is a respectful acknowledgment of the king's generosity and prosperity, but there are no strict policies. Only that you consume freely and joyfully."

Esther nodded, heaving an internal sigh of relief. A part of her found this amusing. When she returned, Mordecai would be astounded at her abundant knowledge of court customs. He would tease her, jest that she was above a common man such as himself. The thought made her smile, though painfully sick for home.

As the rising moon signaled the end of the day's instruction, Esther lowered her head in gratitude to Fatemeh. The older girl returned the gesture with a graceful smile. With her regal stature and crown of braids, Esther wondered why Fatemeh had never been presented as an eligible maiden for the throne. She possessed the composure and wisdom of a thousand queens. Lost in thought, Esther nearly collided with Hegai on her way back to her bedchambers.

"We have a habit of encountering each other at odd hours of the day," he said.

Esther bowed politely. "My apologies. I've just finished with Fatemeh." She smiled up at him. "Her elegance makes her far more suitable for the throne."

Hegai smiled, a strange sight on his typically stern face. "You are eager to downplay yourself. You must have confidence in your abilities, especially as I introduce your other tutors tomorrow."

"Thank you, but my pride is swollen enough," Esther laughed. "I shouldn't fan the flames of that fire."

"I argue that is what the truly humble would say."

She shrugged. "Perhaps you're right, but it's easy to feign humility."

He gazed at her curiously. "I don't believe you would."

"You flatter nicely, Hegai," Esther remarked playfully. "Perhaps it is you who should wear the queen's robes."

The eunuch laughed heartily. Esther started, realizing she had never heard him laugh before. It was a low, pleasant sound.

"I bid you a good night now." He dipped his head slightly. "Rest well. I'll look forward to our instruction tomorrow."

She bowed, a smile gracing her lips. "As will I."

———

"Adara, can I ask you a question?"

"Anything, my lady."

Esther hummed. She focused on stilling her head as Adara weaved an intricate braid. "Do you know what happened to Queen Vashti?"

Adara released a deep sigh, shoving another pin into Esther's hair. "I know as much as you do. His Majesty is not one to divulge secrets to common workers like us, and it is not our place to pry. Why do you ask?"

Esther fidgeted with one of the lip products on her vanity, screwing and unscrewing the vial of pigment. "I just wonder if we could have avoided this entire ordeal. I have always thought Queen Vashti to be the picture of elegance, and she was quite beautiful. I can't imagine King Xerxes banishing her over an insignificant matter."

Adara hummed in thought, lowering her voice. "Well, I have heard rumors that Queen Vashti refused to appear before King Xerxes, and he banished her for disobedience."

Esther's eyes widened as she playfully gasped. "Adara, you *do* know what happened."

She laughed. "I have heard rumors, but I don't know the entire truth. I was told that Queen Vashti fell ill, and with her worsening condition, she refused to present her body before the king and his men." Adara tied the last knot in Esther's braid as she took a step back to admire her handiwork. "But only the gods know what truly happened."

Esther hummed in thought as she smoothed her hand over her thick braid. As Adara walked her to the tutoring room, Esther mused over the version of King Xerxes that Vashti had known. Before the banishment, had he treated her kindly? There seemed to be little room in the court for romance. Was love nothing but a political tool? Xerxes was a deity among his people, powerful and unattainable. She had often heard his name both praised and blasphemed in the streets of Susa. What version of the king would she encounter during their night together?

Esther barely had time to linger in her thoughts before her instruction began. After her morning teachings with Fatemeh, Hegai introduced her to two young men, new tutors sworn to secrecy. There was Azar, her dancing instructor. He extended his hand to her, his fiery red robes sweeping through the air. Reza, who had mastered control over the mind, greeted her with a calculating smile. Their names blurred together initially, slipping through Esther's memory like sand. How was she meant to carry all this knowledge at once, on top of what Fatemeh and Hegai already required of her?

"Don't concern yourself with success," Hegai said when she voiced her anxieties. "We're here to help you. Focus on the process, and the outcome will speak for itself."

Mordecai had always prized Esther's education. He had taught her how to read through sacred writings, but her mind had never been refined to such an intense degree. Days bled into weeks. Esther rose before sunrise to sit with Fatemeh, learning the invisible web of court life: to only speak when spoken to, to lower her gaze in the presence of powerful men, to veil displeasure behind serenity. And slowly, she felt her lessons seeping into her bones beyond the walls of instruction. Her posture straightened without thought, and her steps softened. Her face had become less expressive, more regal. She spoke in level tones. She noticed more about people, the movement of their eyes and hands in conversation.

Meals followed in the courtyard, where Kyra joined her without fail. A routine had formed between them, an unspoken exchange of companionship. Esther derived a strange comfort from Kyra's bluntness, a refreshing beacon amid the complexities of her training.

"What drives you to such honesty?" Esther had asked jokingly after Kyra criticized the thinness of her bracelet. According to her friend, she might as well have tied a string around her wrist.

"Lying to soothe another's vanity is pointless," she replied. "If there was dirt on my nose, I'd much rather someone tell me the truth to scrub it off."

Esther looked forward to those moments, to those morning meals spent in the shade with Kyra as she looked out at the fountains, water rippling under the heat. The breeze whispered through their robes, and the garden's sunrise aroma quieted Esther's mind. It was a space for tranquility before the day's toil.

Esther was drinking from an endless well. Floods of knowledge submerged her, knowledge she never expected to harbor. And her body was changing. She had always walked with a slender frame, but now her legs and shoulders firmed with muscle under Azar's critical eye.

"Are you dancing, or are you swatting insects?" Esther heard far too many times. Azar lifted her head by the chin and straightened her wrists. "Do it again," he said. "This is *Lezgi*. Your fingers should glide through the air, not slice through it."

To Azar's approval, Esther found her steps becoming lighter, her arms floating rather than flailing. She would never forget the first time Azar smiled after a performance. It felt like a hard-earned trophy. But nothing was more fascinating than her evenings with Reza. His understanding of the human condition was astounding in its simplicity.

"We define ourselves through our choices and actions," he said. "Evil defines evil, and good defines good. As queen, your actions define not only yourself but also your people. Choose with discernment."

"What if my decisions put my people in danger?" Esther asked. "That's an enormous pressure. It's impossible to know whether all of my choices are beneficial."

"That's why you must define good according to your own conviction," Reza answered, clasping his hands in front of his torso. "You must find what grounds you, Esther. Find what gives even the smallest actions the greatest meanings. To live any life loosely is worthless, even a royal one."

One night, Esther trudged through the halls of the harem, her feet sore and mind aching. Each step felt heavier than the next, and her eyes blinked with a sluggish weight. The day's work had been especially tiresome. Azar was fond of ripping her muscles to shreds. As Esther drowsily lumbered to her bedchambers, her senses abruptly flashed to alertness as a rushing maiden crashed into her, stumbling to the ground.

"Oh! Are you alright—"

Esther extended her hand to the girl, but she quickly pushed past her, disappearing around the corner in a blur of dark curls.

9

STHER HAD ECLIPSED A CERTAIN POINT IN HER CONSCIOUSNESS** that revealed how much she had changed in such a short amount of time. She was losing track of the months. She felt herself morphing into an unfamiliar creature, someone who powdered her face every morning and straightened her posture at the table. Someone who sucked in her stomach when she walked and donned elaborate dresses daily. Someone who deliberately consumed less to perfect her figure. Someone who was forgetting her culture.

These things may have been thrust upon her, but no matter the cause, the danger of dismantling her identity grew stronger. Did she find more fulfillment in the jewels of her dresses or the pillars of her heritage? Esther could not shake the same pervading questions from her mind: why was she trying so hard? What was this place transforming her into? Perhaps Kyra had been right. Maybe the House of Women did corrupt all that entered through its gilded gates. And yet, every fiber in her being rebelled against the thought of giving up. She couldn't stop now. She loved waking to the sound of her handmaidens' laughter, reveling in her time with Kyra, poking at Hegai's infinite wisdom. Still, this glittering emptiness could not replace her true home.

Night had fallen upon King Xerxes's empire. Stars threaded together along the sky as the moon presided over sleeping souls. Sleeping souls except one. Esther found it impossible to shut her eyes. Her thoughts paced relentlessly through her mind, refusing to grant her rest. Esther tossed the plush blankets off her body, feeling a cold draft hit her skin from the open window. She threw on a coat over her sleeping gown, slowly pushing the door ajar. She strolled through the halls, approaching the back entrance to the outside pavilion.

Esther inhaled deeply, the cool midnight air sending a chill through her body. The courtyard gleamed calmly under the silver moonlight. The grass and fountains and flowers had fallen asleep, transforming the space into a land of dreams.

Esther walked along the edge of the courtyard, running her fingers along the wall of bushes closing the harem off from the rest of the world. The shrubs broke off into a rectangular border surrounding a small gated door. Esther gazed at it longingly. Freedom was just a locked door away.

The sound of pacing footsteps halted her tracks, followed by a rustle in the bushes. She treaded toward the noise, her feet silent against the grass. Had someone seen her? She darted behind the closest tree, peering over the sides. It was coming from outside the harem. Esther knelt low, sneaking closer to the gate. Peeking through the gaps in the bushes, she made out the silhouette of a man. Esther's heart leapt violently, sending electricity straight to her core. She squinted through the nighttime darkness. *Could it be?* There was no mistaking that familiar beard and beige robe, that familiar set of eyes prone to crinkling at the corners upon a smile.

Illusions were driving her to insanity. She only needed to blink a few times before she regained her senses. She closed her eyes, reopened them. But there he was. Esther felt her soul tugging her towards Mordecai. Her Abba, her home. He was pacing back and forth, his body language wrought with distress. What was he doing here? How had he located her?

Esther opened her mouth to cry out to him. After ages of longing for the comfort of his presence, he was *so* close. Without the gate and the wall of leaves, he was just within arm's reach. But something held her back. It would be unwise to interact now, even after months of absence. What if she were caught? *But what if she wasn't?* Esther almost turned away, but the whisper escaped her mouth before she could stop herself.

"Abba!"

Mordecai turned sharply. His eyes widened as he hastened to her, hands clawing at the bushes. "Hadassah," he sobbed quietly. His voice cracked with barely restrained emotion. He fisted the metal rods of the gate and shook them furiously, but the entry didn't budge. Disbelief glistened in his eyes as they locked onto hers.

Mordecai's cheeks looked hollow, almost sickly, but it was undoubtedly his face, his voice. Esther swallowed her tears over the lump in her throat. She had to be strong for him, to show him she was safe. "Abba." She tried reaching for his hand through the gate's small opening, but the gap was too small. This small inability to reach him, this minute cruelty, heightened the stinging behind her eyes.

"Hadassah, I can hardly believe it's you," he said emphatically. "Are you well? Have you been hurt?" He squinted. "I can hardly see you in this moonlight, but you look beautiful. Even more beautiful than you have always been."

Esther smiled, her heart swelling at the familiar rise and fall of his voice. "I've missed you, Abba. I'm more than well." She painted a picture of the abundance of food, the floral scent of the oils, the golden glint of her jewelry, the way each morning ushered itself into her room in a brilliant display of light.

"And this is all to prepare you to meet with King Xerxes?" Mordecai asked.

Esther nodded. "We are allowed one night with him, and then we shall be moved into different quarters."

Mordecai nodded. "Hadassah, promise me you won't stray from who you are."

"I promise."

"Good." Her Abba exhaled. "You know, everything is much dimmer in your absence."

"That's very poetic of you."

"Poetry exaggerates, but my words are sincere." Esther mirrored Mordecai's smile, even as her heart ached at his unfiltered affection. "I trust you have not revealed yourself to anyone?" he inquired.

"No, Abba." Mordecai sighed deeply in relief at her words. "Everyone knows me as Esther, and I suggest you address me in the same way lest someone overhear you."

The padding of footsteps sounded behind her. Esther's head whipped over her shoulder. Someone was running away. Anxiety took root in her stomach, sending flares of panic to her chest.

"I must go before I am seen with you," she said, reliving when she had first been wrestled away. She remembered the rough hands of the guards against her skin, the desperation in Mordecai's eyes. Her spirits plunged into the depths of her gut. She had just been reunited with her only family, and now they had to separate again.

"I will be here again tomorrow night," he said. "But you cannot risk your safety for me. I shall see you soon, Hadassah, regardless of where life takes us."

After assuring Mordecai that she would do everything in her power to see him again, Esther made haste back to the harem's halls. She rushed to her chambers, paranoia festering in her mind like a disease. She was almost certain she had seen the shadow of a person whisk behind her before leaving the courtyard.

———

It's her. It's her. I know it's her.

Zelah darted through the halls, nearly tripping over her feet. Her nose was still cold from exposure to the frigid night air, though she hardly noticed. She had seen her. *Esther.* She had been outside speaking to a man during restricted hours. She finally spotted her target's broad back and dark skin as he patrolled the halls.

"Hegai!" she called.

He snapped to attention at the frantic girl. "Zelah, what are you doing? You should not be out during these hours."

She bowed. "I apologize. I'm aware of my actions, but you should know I am not the only one breaking rules."

He raised an eyebrow. "Oh?"

"Esther was outside in the courtyard talking to a man through the bushes. I am certain."

Zelah kept her voice steady. Remaining calm and collected, just as a queen would. Pursuing justice, just as a queen would. Keeping her opinions to herself, just as a queen would.

Zelah had a growing suspicion that Esther was hiding something, and tonight was even further proof that the girl was not what she seemed. When she had initially passed by her room and heard mutterings in a language she did not know, she was suspicious. Though she couldn't decipher her words, the intonations sounded awfully similar to the Hebrew prayers and conversations she overheard in the streets. But surely an Israelite would not have been selected as one of the king's potential queens. The Jews were foreigners in this land. Though King Xerxes and his father had been more tolerant of their kind, Zelah knew the people of the empire would not embrace a Jew on the throne so easily. And neither would she. The Israelites did not understand the hardships of their people, and they took the king's mercy for granted. To have a foreigner ruling the empire would mean their destruction.

Hegai's face remained stern. "Thank you for letting me know. But I question how you became so familiar with Esther's whereabouts without her knowing or seeing you."

Zelah reddened, though she kept her voice level. "I was merely taking a nighttime stroll, and I stumbled across her briefly."

A slight stretch. Zelah had been unable to sleep, and upon hearing footsteps outside her door, she embarked on an investigation. Recognizing Esther's figure and her steady manner of walking, curiosity blazed in her mind. She needed to expose Esther before she posed a threat to the empire, but Zelah needed evidence. This was the perfect opportunity.

Hegai remained silent. Zelah forced herself to keep her breaths even under his calculating gaze.

"Allow this to be a warning, Zelah. You should not be awake past midnight, and you certainly should not be secretly following any maiden," he said sternly. Outrage and embarrassment sweltered inside her, but her features betrayed nothing. "Whether their conduct is appropriate will be for me to take care of. Now, please," he continued, gesturing to the hallway. "I will escort you back to your room."

Zelah sighed, following the eunuch back to her bedchambers. She sank into her sheets, frustration blazing in her mind. Why was it that she had been admonished instead of Esther? Yes, she had broken some rules, but Esther had broken those rules as well. And beyond that, she had been talking to another man. Perhaps a secret lover? How scandalous.

Zelah forced her eyes closed. In her mind's eye, she saw her ailing sister in bed, her skin sallow where it had once been rosy with life. She thought of her mother selling herself into prostitution, only to barely afford medicine for her fading daughter. She thought of the sleepless nights by her sister's side, regretting that she had not cherished her joy before the sickness consumed it all.

If Zelah were crowned queen, all of her problems would be mended. The court's best healers would care for her sister. With the crown's riches in their hands, her mother would no longer live in misery. Zelah would no longer be caught between the tragedies of her family, stuck in the middle between her sister's ailment and her mother's despair. It was her duty to save her home—her kingdom, her family. And Esther would not get in her way.

———

Esther paced through the halls, her heart threatening to pulse out of her chest. The image of her Abba's face behind the gate's gold-lacquered spirals seared through her mind. The courtyard truly had been a land of dreams. An enormous weight lifted off her shoulders, an affliction she had shouldered since her arrival at the House of Women. She could rest knowing that Mordecai wasn't worlds away from her. He was safe.

Esther commanded her legs to press on faster, scarcely aware of how quickly she was moving until she stumbled into Hegai's back. She drew back at once, startled by the impact. An icy dread unfurled within her as the realization struck. She had disobeyed his rules. *Many* of his rules.

"Oh, Hegai, please forgive me," she said, bowing deeply. "I know I have done wrong."

"I'm aware, Esther."

Her gaze snapped toward his face, searching for any sign of anger. It betrayed nothing, not in the stern line of his mouth or in the onyx of his eyes. *How had he known?*

"Let us go elsewhere," he said. "These empty halls echo the sound of my voice far too much."

He swept them behind the shadow of a corridor into a small library. The room was dark, and the air hung with the must of neglected parchment. The scratching sound of a flame cut through the space as Hegai lit a candle, placing it on a nearby platform. The fire cast a muted glow over Esther's bare arms.

"Now, tell me everything," he said.

Hegai listened intently, pacing the room as she recounted the night. He seemed incapable of remaining in one position for too long. Esther closed her eyes as she described Mordecai's appearance behind the gate, those wide, disbelieving eyes and gaunt cheekbones tormenting her heart. She was careful to avoid his name, lest he be located and punished for speaking to her.

"This man is your relative?" Hegai spoke after considering her words.

"Yes, though he is more of a father to me. I never knew my parents."

"I'm sorry to hear that."

Esther smiled. "It's not your doing, but thank you. I'm sure you can imagine my elation at seeing him."

Hegai hummed deeply. "Regardless of my sentiments, you understand that your actions directly defied my orders."

She tilted her head down, feeling a wave of remorse. Hegai had treated her with incredible kindness, and she had given disobedience in return. "I understand. I'm sorry, Hegai."

"And you understand that I cannot have maidens running around at midnight without supervision?"

"Yes, sir."

Silence settled between them. Esther lowered her gaze to her feet, bracing herself for the final blow. Punishment for her disobedience, Hegai would say. Expulsion from the House of Women would surely follow. How could she have yielded so easily to her impulse? And yet, Esther carried no regret for speaking to Mordecai. That brief exchange had soothed months of longing, months spent wandering in the darkness.

"This man you speak of," Hegai spoke, finally breaking the silence. "His name is Mordecai."

Astonishment slammed into her chest. "How—"

"Your relative is Mordecai, and he works for King Xerxes as a scribe. He has cared for you as one of his own since birth. He cherishes you with an all-consuming love, and he would gladly surrender his life for you."

Esther reared back. "Hegai, how do you know these things?"

"I have become well-acquainted with Mordecai over these past several months. He paces behind that gate every day without fail, waiting for me to assure him of your safety." Hegai clasped his hands together at his torso. His gaze softened as it rested on her. "He will return tomorrow night. If you wish to speak to him one final time, I will personally ensure you are not punished. After that, I cannot allow you to see him again."

Esther's eyes widened, her heart soaring with hope. "Hegai, you cannot do such a thing for me."

He shook his head. "Promise that you will remain in the harem and abide by my rules. I can only extend so much mercy, even to you."

Esther bowed deeply to the ground. "You have my word."

They walked the length of the corridor in silence, a quiet strangely touched by peace. The hush felt almost companionable, broken only by the muted echo of their footsteps along the polished stone. The light of lanterns flickered against the walls as they passed, casting slow shadows across the expanse.

Once they arrived at her bedchamber doors, Esther sank to the ground again in a deep bow.

"My lips are becoming accustomed to thanking you," she said softly. "Good night, Hegai."

He inclined his head in return. "Good night, my lady."

IO

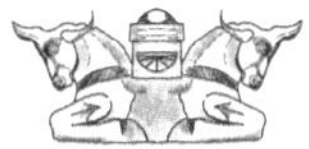

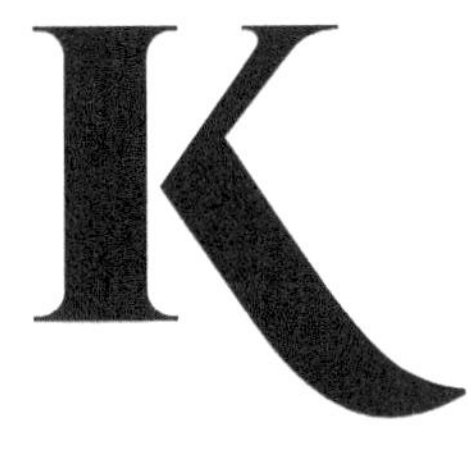**ING XERXES SAT IN HIS STUDY,** cradling his head in his hands. He was the King of Kings. The Vessel of the Gods. Rings of gold weighed his fingers down, and each breath he took curled with divinity.

He should have been untouchable. Yet his dominion proved worthless against his thoughts. Paranoia had mercilessly gnawed at his conscience since the dawn of Queen Vashti's banishment. Xerxes was no stranger to the spell of wine. Intoxication was not at fault—his decision had stemmed from rationality. Indeed, anger sweltered in his chest when he recalled Vashti's disobedience. No one defied the supreme ruler, and Vashti should have understood her duty of submission. What had sparked her defiance? She knew the consequences of challenging the king. Banishment was an act of mercy. So why couldn't he shake his unease?

His people were partly to blame. Vashti's expulsion had done nothing to bolster his already tainted image. He knew his subjects thought ill of him. He heard the whispers, tones that only grew louder with each passing day. He was the reckless son who failed to live up to his father's name: Darius I, a true military hero. Someone people could put their faith in.

Look where he ended up, Xerxes thought bitterly. Humiliated by the Greeks and bedridden from disease. It had not taken long for the mighty Darius to be reduced to a withering corpse.

Xerxes had inherited not only his father's throne, but his father's failures. He had inherited a war. His only choice was to avenge his father, to preserve the empire. To finally prove he was worthy of praise. Xerxes would restore order where his father could not. Darius had failed in his battle at Marathon, years of planning gone to waste in an unfinished outpouring of blood. Xerxes had long surrendered hope for negotiations with the Athenians. They were unmovable in their rebellion against him, raising their fists in that blasphemous parade of independence. It came as no surprise when his spies reported their emerging battle plans against his armies.

Sighing, Xerxes massaged his forehead with the tips of his fingers. His anguish was creeping into his outer appearance. Just that morning, he had examined himself in the mirror, hardly believing the dark circles and pale skin in the glass belonged to him. He hoped the color would return to his face once he began meeting Hegai's virgins. The time to replace Vashti was fast approaching, yet he still had not determined the woman he desired. His union with Vashti had been arranged. Many women could throw him into pleasure, but few could rule at his right hand. Fewer still could restore the people's faith in his reign. The realization sat heavily in his chest. The weight of the crown felt greater on his head. A sudden knock broke the stillness of the chamber, wrenching him from his thoughts.

"Come in."

Haman, his highest court official, swept into the room with a stack of scrolls in his arms. He bowed in one swift motion. His scar appeared darker in the room's dimness.

"Good evening, Your Majesty," he said. "A scribe handed me some reports that must be reviewed as soon as possible."

Xerxes unraveled the scrolls, his eyes glazing over the words. Something about Thessaly offering troops for weapons. Was that also something about Thebes? Each word added another weight on his eyelids, and he did not try to mask his exhaustion.

"Haman."

"Yes, Your Majesty?"

Xerxes tapped his stylus against the desk. "If you were the king of Persia, what sort of queen would you seek?"

The younger man placed his hands thoughtfully behind his back. "My opinion does not measure up to yours, Your Highness. Still, I would desire someone undeniably beautiful. There is great power in beauty. If she does not reflect Your Majesty's divine favor, then she is not worthy of a crown."

Xerxes dismissed Haman with a wave of his hand. He needed time to think. And perhaps some wine.

After calling for a goblet of that notorious red elixir, he retired to his bedchambers. Tomorrow, there would be a large council among the generals to discuss the Athenians. But tonight he was to forget, to turn himself over to numbness.

A small voice in his soul cried out to him. It clasped its invisible hands and begged on its knees. Stop, it said. Stop before you wander too far, before you destroy yourself. *I can't*, he replied. His answer never changed. *I can't.* A spirit of desolation had possessed him, forcing him to hold an empty cup that could not be filled, not by all the wine of his stores nor all the jewels of the earth.

The King of Kings took another swig of wine, crawled under the sheets, and shut his eyes.

———

The air of the council chamber was cool despite the heat of the midday sun. Stone columns soared up to the heavens, their shadows stretching along the marble floor. Xerxes sat on a raised golden dais. He gripped his scepter, motionless as he gazed out upon his assembly of generals. Maps lay unfurled around the circle of men in harsh sketches of the Aegean sea. Athens was marked in red pigment, the lines around it pressed deep, as though the stylus had lingered there longer than necessary.

"The Athenians rely on their fleet," General Artabanus said, pressing a finger into the coastline. "They will not meet us on open land unless forced."

"Their numbers are few," General Morteza added. "We have historically enforced order in our provinces through the vastness of our armies. The Athenians may be clever, but even they will submit to an overwhelming force."

"It's not that simple," Artabanus interjected. "We cannot underestimate their spirit. The Athenians know our strength lies in numbers. It may be wise to consider the traps that await our fleets should we rely on brute force alone."

"The gods have blessed us with abundance in all things," Xerxes said, breaking his silence. "We must quench the spirit of rebellion that has infected the Athenians with defiance. General Morteza, I command you and General Artabanus to lead two-thirds of our fleets into the coastline."

Xerxes traced his finger along the map, the parchment smooth against his skin. "You will show no mercy."

"Your Majesty," Artabanus began. "It may be wise to consider—"

"My decision is final." Xerxes's voice rippled in resounding waves throughout the chamber. He struck the end of his scepter against the ground. "You will bring glory to the throne."

The generals nodded and returned to the map. Murmurs rippled throughout the room as strategy layered atop strategy in vengeance for Marathon—crude depictions of endless fleets, arrows marking unpredictable winds, and dotted lines of shrewd supply lines. Then, without warning, another sound echoed in the room. Footsteps. Getting closer. Faster. Louder.

A young court official crossed the threshold of the chamber without announcement. His sandals scraped the marble floor, loud as a shout in a sea of quiet. The generals froze. The boy stopped short, color draining from his face as he realized where he stood.

"Your Majesty," he began, breathless. "Forgive me for this imprudence, but there is urgent news from the western satrap—"

Xerxes lifted his eyes, clenching the golden scepter in his hand until his knuckles whitened. The generals faced the king, a knowing look darkening their grave faces.

"Young man," Xerxes began. His voice was level, cold. "Do you have any experience in the military?"

A flash of confusion appeared on the boy's face before he lowered his eyes. "No, Your Highness. I am only a scribe."

Xerxes tapped his finger against the orb of his scepter slowly. "And you understand that any man who approaches the king unannounced is a crime punishable by death?"

"Your Majesty, I was ordered to approach you regardless—"

"General Morteza," Xerxes continued. "On the day of the invasion of Athens, place this boy on the front lines unarmed and untrained. You will send him out before the Athenians, and none of your troops will assist him. Any trace of disobedience will send you and your men into an early grave."

"Understood, Great King."

The silence in the room was electric. Xerxes turned to the guards by his side, gesturing for them to take the young scribe away. The boy cried out desperately, thrashing against the grip of the king's eunuchs. His shouts soon faded into an echo as he was dragged further out through the hall.

"Now," King Xerxes placed the golden scepter in his lap. The metal was cool against the fabric of his robes. He folded his hands in front of him, returning to his generals. Their mouths set in grim lines. "Where were we?"

II

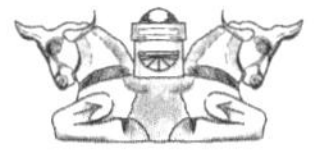

EGAI WAS A MAN OF KEEN
AWARENESS. His mind was never
still. In a crowded room, his eyes leapt
from person to person, catching on to
smiles that didn't reach the eyes, hands
that came to life in conversation,
lingering gazes on passing beauties. In the House of Women,
he noticed other things. He noticed the chime of silver bangles
against wrists and the aroma of oils. The shrieking whispers of
gossip and the glint of feminine eyes sparking salacious desires
in the minds of men.

Hegai also noticed Esther.

She was quiet, almost invisible in her silence, but not
fragile. When she spoke, he felt a draw to lean closer. She
moved with an air of sincerity and a graceful ease, each step
lighter than the last. Perhaps most fascinating was her smile. It
was not one of upturned lips but of gleaming eyes.

Beyond his observations, he had learned much about her through Mordecai, her unrelenting father. His nightly ritual had begun on the second day of the virgins' arrival. Mordecai's sandals crunched against the ground as he paced behind the gate, muttering to himself. Hegai had been quick to dismiss him. There was no time to entertain the whims of a strange old man. But curiosity had struck Hegai when, at the next moonrise, the man had returned. And then the next night. And the next night. And the night after that.

"State your business," Hegai had finally stated, irritated at his persistence. "You are not welcome here."

"Please," Mordecai had replied, his voice choking with desperation. "My name is Mordecai, and I only want to inquire after the safety of my daughter. I was told to come here."

Hegai shook his head. "I cannot help you. I will ask you one last time to leave these grounds before you are forced off."

Hegai turned, preparing to walk away from him.

"Her name is Esther."

At this point, Hegai had become increasingly curious about Esther. She had noticed the art on the wall, a tribute to the king created years ago by an Israelite painter. The Jewish style was unrecognizable to the Persians—no one noticed the art on the wall. He paused, slowly turning back.

"You are Esther's guardian?"

The old man nodded fervently.

"Esther is safe."

"How can I know your words are true?" Mordecai replied, the moonlight illuminating the anguish in his gaze.

"I speak by the authority of King Xerxes," Hegai said. "I swear by His Majesty's throne that Esther is being cared for."

Hegai would never forget the pure relief that washed over Mordecai's face. Tears formed at the corners of his eyes as he thanked the eunuch profusely. Hegai was almost envious of the old man. His brothers had rejected him once he pledged allegiance to King Xerxes, a king they believed guilty of betrayal—a betrayal of their people by upholding Darius's toleration for the Jews. The pain of their hate pierced his heart to the core. But time had taken its course. Hegai forgot them, even the sound of their voices. Mordecai's deep affection reminded him of a distant memory, the memory of his bygone family.

Twilight had descended on the land. Hegai watched the flames of the corridor's braziers dance with life in the darkness as he waited for Esther to emerge from her bedchambers. Hegai had promised to escort her to the courtyard to meet Mordecai secretly. He knew he was breaking the law. It was his duty to supervise the maidens and ensure order, not encourage them into disobedience. His mind berated him, but he could not defy the instinct of his heart.

Hegai finally caught sight of her. Her eyes were twinkling under the cloak draped over her head.

"Thank you, Hegai," she said, bowing low in greeting.

He waved his hand. "Your gratitude is growing tiresome. You need not thank me so much." He gestured to the hall. "Come, follow me."

Esther joined in step beside him. "It would be improper not to express my gratitude."

"Consider them favors for a friend."

Esther's smile brightened. "You consider me a friend?"

"Let's press on, Esther."

"Do you truly mean that?"

"Are you hard of hearing?"

"I ought to be grateful that the emotionless guardian of this place has found a companion in me," she said with an upturn of her lips.

"I may rescind my friendship if you continue to talk."

Esther laughed, a melody cascading out of her lips.

They finally arrived at the back entrance to the courtyard. Esther pulled the cloak farther over her face as Hegai unlocked the door with a swift *click*.

"Be quick," he warned. "I'll remain here until you return."

The nighttime chill swirled around Hegai as Esther hastened past him, her cloak blending into the darkness. Hegai turned his gaze away as she enveloped Mordecai in a fierce embrace. The moment seemed too private for his eyes. He shouldn't have even allowed her to see him. It was unfair to the other maidens. He should have felt remorseful, even the slightest pinch of regret. But hearing their faint cries of excitement, even Hegai couldn't contain the smile that eclipsed his face.

———

Esther had returned to the paradise of her dreams. She gazed out at the familiar lush greenery, relishing in the cool grass between her toes. A breeze whispered around her body as she spun in an elegant white gown, its hem swirling around her legs in an enchanting ring.

She marveled at the ground as more myrtle flowers erupted from the grass, forming a trail deeper into the landscape. Esther followed the path, watching gleefully as new flowers blossomed with each step she took. Her walk turned into a run as she laughed, joyfully in stride with the life surrounding her. The flowers led to another pomegranate tree, twice as large as the others in the garden. Its fruit appeared even more succulent, hanging from the branches as if begging to be enjoyed.

Esther reached for the pomegranate, cracking it open with the edge of a stone. The seeds glistened in the fruit's deep red casing. She grabbed a handful of seeds and poured them into her mouth. Juice coated her tongue in the sweetest taste—they were even more marvelous than she had remembered. The seeds were so candied, so crunchy, so satiating, so—

Hot? Esther clapped a hand over her mouth, gasping in great heaves as the pomegranate tumbled out of her palm. Her mouth burned. The pain grew hotter and hotter, as if she had swallowed a flaming torch. Her lips felt like she had kissed the sun, scorching and utterly overpowering. Her heart was throbbing, threatening to rip out of her flesh. The world was spinning faster. The pounding in her head was drilling her skull to dust. Esther cried out and collapsed to the ground, clutching at the cool grass for the slightest reprieve.

A hand on her shoulder. Esther gasped as she returned to reality. She clenched her chest to quell the phantom burn. She could still taste the fire in her mouth. Esther breathed deeply, forcing her mind to calm. It was just a dream.

Hegai stood near her bedside, his hands clasped behind him. The lines of his face appeared graver than usual. "Esther, you have been released from the selection," he said flatly. "You will come to the courtyard at once."

Esther's heart stopped. She rubbed her hands over her face, forcing herself to regain full consciousness. Perhaps she had misheard from her grogginess. But there was no mistaking his words. Released from the selection? Did this mean she could return home? Esther was surprised to find that she wasn't thrilled at the prospect of returning to the city streets. She was confused, even disheartened. What had she done wrong? Esther almost opened her mouth to protest. She trusted Hegai. They had even conceded friendship to one another—surely she could speak freely. But upon assessing the severity of his features, Esther realized there was no room for resistance. She was being released from the harem.

She nodded, emerging from her sheets. "As you say, Hegai." Esther bowed deeply. "Thank you for the care I was given."

He nodded once, leaving her chambers. Esther looked around the room. She had nothing to pack—she had arrived at the House of Women with nothing in hand. And now her time was over. Esther made her way to the courtyard, surprised at the small throng of maidens. There must have been twenty of them, Zelah standing among the crowd. No sight of Kyra. Some girls wept openly, and Esther overheard others whisper plans of returning to the harem—whom to beg, the pleasures they could offer to those in power, which doors to knock on.

Each head snapped to Hegai as he stepped onto a raised stone dais, gesturing for the maidens to quiet. He motioned orders at the other eunuchs as they arranged the maidens in a line. Esther suddenly remembered Mardonius, the official who had questioned them in her first test. Was this also a test? Esther tensed when she was positioned at the end of the procession next to Zelah, her angled chin pointing slightly upward. Esther held her breath, fixing her gaze forward.

Hegai approached the first maiden. "Why do you believe you've been dismissed?"

Esther couldn't hear her answer, but she saw Hegai nod in approval. He approached each maiden one by one. Esther's nerves buzzed frantically as he approached closer and closer.

Hegai finally stood before Zelah, posing the same question. She lifted her chin slightly higher.

"I don't believe I've truly been dismissed," Zelah began. "I have behaved according to all that you have taught us."

Hegai's face was a blank map as he nodded. He then faced Esther. "Why do you believe you've been dismissed, Esther?"

"My understanding does not measure up to your wisdom." Esther looked up into the eunuch's eyes. "But if I have ever made the mistake of trusting myself above the crown, then I will walk out of this place of my own volition."

Her heart hurt at the coldness of his stare. Had their connection meant nothing to him? Had his friendship been a farce, just another test of her worth? Hegai nodded curtly before returning to the stone platform, facing the maidens. "This was a test of accepting difficult circumstances." There it was again. *A test.* "Let this be a warning that you will be released if you do not measure up to the royal standard. You may return to your chambers."

A slight relief washed over her, but waves of guilt and sorrow quickly dominated it. She should want to return home. She had been away for far too long, away from Mordecai, away from Leila, away from her people. And yet, the idea of leaving the harem felt like a defeat she couldn't accept. Then there was Hegai. What did he truly think of her? If this had been a test all along, then why regard her with such distance?

As Esther walked through the courtyard back to her chambers, her eyes lingered on the myrtle flowers sprouting from the bushes. She placed a hand on her chest, remembering the pain that had sprung forth from the poisoned pomegranate in her dream. Something was deeply unsettling about the idea of poison in a paradise. Was her dream meant to be a warning? A reminder that people were not always as they appeared? Esther closed her eyes as she sank back into her sheets, feeling the heaviness of slumber tug on her eyelids. She drifted off, hoping she wouldn't return to that gilded paradise.

———

It was unusually cold. Esther shed her warm blankets, the chill gnawing at her nose and bare arms. Her eagerness was immeasurable as the steam from the freshly drawn bath breathed on her skin, enveloping her in warmth.

Elina rubbed oils into her palms, working her fingers through Esther's hair. "We're ordered to lather these oils on you, my lady, but even I think this is excessive."

"How often are you drowned in these scents?" Nava chimed in from the vanity.

"Multiple times every day," Esther replied with a smile.

"If they add one more oil to your skin," Elina continued. "You'll slide straight out of the harem."

"Then at least I'll leave smelling heavenly."

Nava hummed. "A heavenly smell and a very expensive smear on the marble."

Laughter filled the bathhouse, ringing along the tiled walls. Esther readied herself for the day as if donning armor. Two careful strokes of kohl darkened her eyes. She slid a stack of gold bangles down her wrist, the metal clinking softly with each movement.

The morning air nipped at her hands as she stepped from her chambers. She stopped short, rearing in surprise. Hegai stood waiting just beyond the doorway, their eyes locking together. The walls in her mind rose. The sharp coldness she had seen in his eyes the night before was gone, but the memory of his hostility lingered.

"Esther," he said gently, extending his arm. "Allow me to escort you."

She dipped her head in greeting, hesitantly placing her hand upon his forearm.

They strode together in silence, their steps echoing in the open hallways.

"I wanted to apologize for last night," he finally said. "I can imagine what you must have thought of me."

Esther shook her head quickly. "You were doing your duty. I understand." The distance in her tone betrayed her.

Hegai glanced at her from the corner of his eye. "I could not show partiality to you before the others, Esther. As much as it pained me to treat you coldly, it kept you from becoming a target."

Esther released a quiet breath. "I know. Truly, I do." She paused, fingers tightening slightly against his arm. "I suppose I was dismayed to feel as though our connection had mattered to me alone."

Hegai smiled. Such a rare sight, warm and unguarded. It softened the severity of his features, melting his onyx irises. "Believe me. I would be a fool to disregard someone like you."

Esther felt her heart ease, assurance taking root where hurt had dwelled. *Someone like you.* Mordecai's words suddenly appeared in her mind, a fragment of their exchange the night Hegai had allowed her to see him.

"Abba, what am I to do?" she had whispered under the moonlit sky. "Everything about this compromises what you taught me and what our people stand for. I am being prepared to rule a land that worships statues and winged goddesses. At every table, there is food I cannot eat. And—" her voice had faltered. "I am expected to lie with the king. You know our law forbids this. What am I to do?" She murmured her last words as a question to herself, a question that had never left her mind.

She had expected judgment, even condemnation. But no, Mordecai had looked at her with soft eyes, eyes that felt like home after months of excruciating exile.

"Do not be afraid, Esther," he spoke gently. "You have been placed here for a reason. Perhaps that reason is not yet known to us, but we must trust that it exists." He swept a hand

over her cheek, brushing the single tear she allowed to fall from her eyes.

"And my faith," he said softly, "rests easily in someone like you."

Esther breathed deeply. She clung to those words like a rope over an abyss, but doubt crept into her conscience. Mordecai declared his faith in her heart, but she wondered if he was misplacing his trust. Who was she to determine right from wrong? She could come to regret the decisions she made. Would she know what to do when her night with King Xerxes fell upon her shoulders? Maybe she was doomed to wallow in shame for the rest of her life.

Hegai pulled her from her thoughts as she was released into the gathering of maidens before the courtyard fountain. She quickly settled at Kyra's side, watching as Hegai raised his hands in a motion of silence.

"Your time with King Xerxes is fast approaching," his voice rumbled. "You all have prepared diligently for this moment. Please follow me."

Her heart dropped. *Already?* Whispers flitted among the ladies, their hushed astonishment mirroring the disbelief in Esther's chest. The throng of maidens trailed behind Hegai into an unexplored hall of the harem, the walls made of pure sandstone. The motifs were minimalistic and barely visible in the dim lighting, a rare aesthetic in the abundant opulence.

They stopped at a magnificent set of double doors, inlaid with golden incisions and precious stones.

Reaching for a key in the pocket of his tunic, Hegai turned the lock and swung the doors open. Esther's eyes widened. Gold. Stacks and stacks of it glittering under the light bouncing off the walls. Fine dresses, bottles of perfume, and extravagant jewelry lay in quantities like sand pebbles along the shore. The maidens gasped, the sheen of the wealth reflecting in their wide gazes.

"I think they could use a little more gold," Kyra snickered, eliciting a smile out of Esther.

"Each of you may take as much as you desire from this treasury to bring with you to the king," Hegai explained. "Remember that you will be sent to a different harem after your encounter. But, for now, please take freely."

He didn't need to say another word. The maidens crowded into the treasury, giddy under the intoxication of precious gems and fineries. They heaved dresses into their arms, lathered their wrists in scented oil. Necklaces were held up to necks, each stone sparkling with ever-shifting flashes of white. A grand reward for the year's hard work. Esther looked at the gaudy chains and sheer bodices in the hands of the other maidens, watching as they held fabrics against their slender frames in fits of giggles.

Esther smiled as Kyra entered the treasury, amused at her fixation on a pair of silver earrings. Hegai observed the maidens as they ravaged through the riches, his face blank in that characteristic stone-cold canvas. Esther ran her hand along the silks and glittering objects that lay before her, utterly clueless. She had been taught how to paint her face to perfection, how to layer silks in a manner befitting her figure. But she hadn't the faintest clue as to King Xerxes's preferences.

"Hegai, what would you have me select?" she asked.

He raised an eyebrow. "This is a matter of personal taste. I'm not a connoisseur of what flatters female vanity."

Esther laughed. "Perhaps not, but you are knowledgeable in what the king likes. I trust your judgment. So," she gestured to the treasury, "what would you have me choose?"

He hummed in thought, playing with the golden rings along his finger.

"With the disobedience of the former queen," he began as they entered the treasury together. "I suspect he would appreciate someone authentic. Select what you believe flatters the most humble, most beautiful parts of yourself. Something—"

He suddenly paused, reaching for a dress hanging over a series of wooden chests. He held up the pristine white silk, studying the subtle golden pattern running down the hem of the gown. The neckline was cut in a deep V-shape, complementing the sleeveless drapery. Though it contrasted the other dresses with their vibrant colors and floral patterns, Esther was quite smitten with it. The gown was simple, but not plain. Elegant, but not extravagant.

"Something like this," Hegai relented a smile. "And perhaps a subtle accessory to complement it."

After perusing the various objects in the treasury, Hegai selected a thin necklace with a glittering gem at the center. He was quick to hand her a perfume bottle, the subtlest scent of lavender emanating from the glass.

"Are you certain you're not an expert in the woes of women?" Esther asked cheekily. "These are beautiful. Perhaps you should have instructed me on how to dress as queen."

"I'm beginning to regret our companionship."

"Surely you don't mean that."

"I only mean that it is not my taste that makes those objects appealing," he continued, nodding toward the objects in Esther's hand. "It is the wearer who makes them becoming."

A smile broke out on Esther's face. "For someone who no longer wants my friendship, you certainly know how to pamper me with compliments."

"Should you become queen, I hope my compliments will warrant a grand royal reward from you."

Esther laughed, though something within her faltered. She had never entertained the idea of royalty before, but now, with her night before King Xerxes fast approaching, the thought crawled into her mind. Of course, it was unlikely. Nearly one hundred maidens had been gathered into the harem. But if she were, would she ever return home? Would she ever see Mordecai again?

She shook her head, dispelling the thought before it could take root. Now was not the time to wander down such paths. Whether chosen or dismissed, she would see her Abba again.

She had to believe that.

12

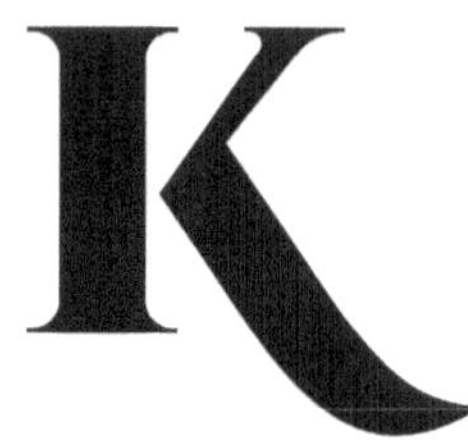YRA WAS GONE. Hegai had whisked her away to the king's chambers in the night, the first maiden chosen to lie with the king. Her absence struck Esther in fragments—she had not realized how thoroughly Kyra filled her days until every hour seemed to echo without her. In the beauty chambers, there was no voice beside her whispering jokes about the oils or the severe faces of the servants. During meals, the seat at her side remained untouched, the platters of fruit no longer shared between them. Even in the gardens, where laughter had bubbled in abundance above them, Esther now walked in quiet solitude.

Would Kyra be suitable as queen? Esther wondered. Her friend was prone to speaking out of turn, bold where others were cautious, yet she carried herself with the effortless confidence of royalty. She would surely win the favor of the court. Of the people, too. Kyra had a gift for shaping words into something alluring, something that lingered in the air long after she had spoken. And she was beautiful, strikingly beautiful. Her umber skin glowed like warm bronze, and her hair framed her face in sculpted perfection, always arranged with meticulous care.

"Esther, what do you believe is the cost of being queen?" Kyra had once asked in the courtyard at night, unwinding from the day's work by the myrtle bushes. They sat with their backs against a tree, relishing in the cool night air brushing past their faces.

"I ought to be asking you that question," Esther replied. She ran her fingers through the blades of grass gently brushing against her leg.

"I want that crown, Esther. I desire it more than anything in this world." Kyra laughed bitterly. "Sounds selfish, doesn't it? But I don't want the crown for its jewels. I want to make my family regret giving up on me. I want them to taste my power after they sold me into this wretched prison."

"Then why ask about the cost of your endeavor?" Esther gazed intently at her friend. "If vengeance is what you truly seek, then I imagine any sacrifice would be worth it."

Silence stretched between them. Esther remembered studying Kyra, the emotion in her eyes contrasting the droop in her shoulders. Despite all the time they had spent together,

Esther realized there were many things about Kyra she still didn't know. She seemed to harbor an immense grief, one that had never been unearthed. Would she don a mask of happiness in front of the king, hoping that marriage would remedy all of her problems?

As the number of remaining maidens thinned with each passing night, Esther's anxiety grew like a parasite. Her time was visible over the horizon, the moment she had sacrificed a year to prepare for. When she first arrived at the House of Women, the queen's crown was the least of her desires. After all, the crown had stolen her from Mordecai. But now royalty sauntered through her mind with the appeal of *reward*. For the past year, she had thrown herself into the kiln of training, heated and refined and hardened into the character of a ruler. To emerge from the fire as a complete sculpture only to return to the soft pot of clay seemed wasteful.

But there was her heart to consider, and her heart pricked her with guilt like a thorn. How could she think so selfishly? Her one wish was to see Mordecai again and return to her home in the city. That was all she needed. In any case, that was likely to be her fate. With women like Kyra, even Zelah, in the pool of King Xerxes's choices, Esther hardly stood a chance. It wasn't wise to consider the outcome, especially considering she had not even encountered King Xerxes yet.

King Xerxes. The King of Kings, Supreme Majesty of the Land. She was expected to pleasure the most powerful man in the kingdom, someone with the world at his feet. He hardly seemed real. Esther was young. Unmarried and inexperienced. Not meant to be with any man, according to Hebrew tradition, unless on the marriage bed. How could she surrender herself, even to the king, and defy the laws she cherished so dearly? The tradition Mordecai had raised her on was the compass to her life, and now she was being forced to veer off course.

Mordecai had placed his faith in her, but a fear encroached her heart that quickened her pulse in random bursts. Sometimes she forgot how to breathe. Panic was a rebellious creature, and it always seemed to arrive at the same thought: there was no way to guarantee she would know what to do. Panic came and went as it pleased, possessing her with anxiety at the most inopportune moments.

And so it arrived. Hegai straightened his posture, gesturing at his body. "When you present yourself before the king, you must always—"

Panic. *I won't know what to do.* Esther slowly lowered herself to the ground, her breath coming in short, sharp snaps. She placed her hand on her chest, zeroing in on the stability of her touch to quell the growing dizziness. She closed her eyes, her heart pounding deafeningly in her ears. Her hand was an anchor point. She was coming back, coming back.

"Esther!" Hegai rushed to her side, placing a hand on her shoulder. His palm was warm, another anchor point to cling to. "Are you alright?"

Esther exhaled sharply, trying to yank herself out of the spell. She shook him off, rising shakily back to her feet. "I'm sorry, Hegai. Please continue."

"What troubles you?"

"Nothing. I'm alright."

He shot her a pointed look. "What is the point of a lie when no one believes it?"

Esther released a long breath, leaning against the wall for support. She didn't speak until her voice returned with steadiness. "I'm worried about my night with King Xerxes."

"Why should you fear? He would be very pleased with you."

Esther fidgeted with her hands. How could she confide in Hegai without revealing her Jewish heritage? As much as she trusted him, she couldn't break her promise to Mordecai. "I'm worried that I won't know the right path to take when I encounter him."

"You fail to trust your own judgment?"

Esther nodded. Hegai hummed in response, tapping his stylus against the desk.

"Do not be overcome by your anxieties," he continued. "You have learned at a pace that surpasses anyone else I have instructed. I do not believe someone who truly doubts themselves would progress so quickly, both in knowledge and in character."

The storm in her mind calmed. She drew a breath, smiling up at him. "You always seem to know the right thing to say. Thank you."

"Of course." His face remained stern, though his voice had taken a softer edge. "Let's return to work. Learning can be a wonderful distraction."

A wonderful distraction indeed. Esther's gaze never strayed from the eunuch. She channeled all of her energy into heeding the rise and fall of his voice.

"Everything I have taught you is important," Hegai asserted. "But you must remember to *never* step out of line. You only approach the king when he summons you. Anyone who comes before him without a summons, be noble or peasant, will be put to death. He may show mercy by extending his golden scepter to you, but it is not worth risking your life." Hegai gazed at her intently. "You must abide by these words, Esther. You are subject to the king at all times. Do you understand?"

"I understand."

———

King Xerxes was tiring of these games. He had hoped that his nighttime affairs with the maidens would take his mind off the wars, that ecstasy would overpower his distress. But he was only left feeling more exhausted, more stripped to the bone.

The maidens were undoubtedly beautiful. For two weeks, he had dined and slept with a new beauty each night. Once the curtains fell with shadows and the candlelight flickered at his bedside, another woman entered the chamber with swaying hips and shining chains. It was becoming monotonous. He hardly remembered their faces at the night's end. Pleasure exploded in a burst, then it was gone. There was something about their desperate crazes to please him that made the intimacy unsatisfying, even artificial. The first lady had been enchanting, but her bold spirit reminded Xerxes of Vashti's rebellion. She wouldn't do. And neither would any of the others. They lacked refinement, and they tasted sourly of vulgarity.

King Xerxes sighed as he sat on a plush carpet in his chambers. A table of food stood before him as he awaited the next maiden. He would find someone suitable. He was sure of it. He had to be. He dared not consider the alternative in which none of the maidens pleased him and left his kingdom incomplete. But Xerxes trusted Hegai more than that—surely his guidance had shaped one woman into his bride.

A knock sounded at the door. The woman sauntered into the room in a wine-red dress, her bronze skin and slender frame exposed. The sheer fabric outlined the shadows of her waist. Jewelry lined her arms and neck and ankles, a shimmering array of silver. She reeked of perfume, the sickly sweet kind that could be alluring in small doses, but it lathered on her skin like water in a bath.

"Good evening, Great King," she said, bowing low to the ground. Her chest peaked above the thin fabric, necklace jangling at her collarbone.

Xerxes returned the bow. "Good evening, my lady."

She was beautiful, perhaps more beautiful than most. The waves of her hair reminded him of Vashti's, but this was not the queen of Persia. Her greatest offering was one night of pleasure, not years of peace. He plastered a smile onto his face, gesturing for her to sit.

Xerxes tried to revel in the thrill of her touch, but a numbness incessantly pervaded his soul. It felt like his empire, his people, were being pulled away farther and farther from his grasp. There was a veil over his eyes, and he didn't know how to regain his sight. He despised how the hollowness made the pleasure less pleasurable, made the wine less satisfying, made the power of his position less gratifying.

Xerxes breathed in her perfume, the sickly sweetness clouding his mind. He hadn't even learned her name.

The King of Kings closed his eyes, pushing his anxiety down to the depths of his soul. He willed himself empty.

13

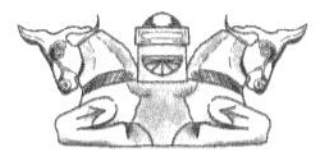

HERE IS A UNIQUE SORT OF RESTLESSNESS that accompanies a day equally anticipated and dreaded. The heart rises and falls, quickens with expectancy and dulls with doom.

The day rose in glorious light. Esther sat in her sheets, gazing at the sky through her window. By this time tomorrow, she would have already encountered the king, and he would have made up his mind about her. The night before, Hegai had spoken the fated words. *He will see you tomorrow night.* Sleep never arrived. She tossed and turned, eyelids shut but nerves alight.

Each hour of training had been another rock leading to the mountain peak. Her body was primed to suit a queenly figure, her face painted to exude queenly beauty, and her mannerisms whipped into grace to honor a queenly audience. She had morphed into another creature.

Her handmaidens wasted no time. Crowding around her, their hands became a storm of productivity. Esther's skin was rubbed raw, her hair braided back until not a single strand rebelled.

"How are you feeling, my lady?" Zarine asked as she dabbed her face with powder.

Esther hid her heaviness behind a smile. "I've never been more nervous in my life."

"What are you afraid of?" Elina replied from the closet as she rummaged through the dresses. "You have nothing to fear."

"A bit of everything, I suppose," Esther said. "The king himself, what I shall do when we meet, the aftermath of our encounter." Her voice sounded distant even to her own ears, her mind absorbed in her anxieties alone. *Will I know what to do?*

Adara hummed, perfecting the shape of her braids. Esther's hair had grown out during her time at the harem, and now it took much longer to style. "Elina is right, my lady," she added. "Your worries are unfounded. We all have faith in your character."

"Besides," Nava added, "I'm sure the king will be quite taken with you. Especially after we finish working our magic." Her voice took on a playful edge as she winked.

Esther slipped into the elegant white gown Hegai had selected for her in the treasury. She touched the glass of the mirror with her fingertips. The drapery folded like a column in elegant lines down her hips. Each movement of her body sent a wave of glimmers over the golden trim of the neckline and waist. A sheer overthrow spilled down her shoulders, concealing her arms in delicate lace. She clipped the silver necklace under her braids, the gem like a teardrop between her clavicles. Scented oil was dabbed lightly on her wrists.

"You look like a queen, my lady," Adara said with a smile.

Esther bowed to her maidens before opening the windows and stepping out onto the balcony. The preparations to embellish her had crept into the afternoon. The sun shone through the window warmly, as if assuring Esther it was watching over her. The rays seeped into her skin, warmth spreading along her bare arms and face. She exhaled. Her thoughts were still a mess, but the sunlight loosened something tight in her chest.

"We were told that you are to continue your usual activities today," Nava spoke. "You'll be summoned back to your chambers early to ensure everything is perfect for His Majesty."

"We wish you luck, my lady," Adara said. "Do not fear, and may the gods be with you."

The time had come. Esther sat before her vanity in silence. Final brushes of pigment whispered against her cheeks. She stood, the hem of her dress tugged to perfection. It was not long before Esther heard a knock at the door. *Hegai.* She embraced her maidens before stepping out the door, her heart pounding with the speed of a thousand chariots.

"Are you ready, Esther?" Hegai asked. Esther placed a palm on his extended arm.

"You have prepared me to great heights."

He smiled. "You have nothing to fear."

The walk to the king's chambers felt endless, each step stretching into its own small eternity. And yet, a journey had never passed faster. Esther could scarcely keep pace with her own heartbeat as they passed through corridor after corridor. She was inside the palace now, the grand dwelling of kings and queens, where gold gleamed as abundantly as wheat in a field. Towering pillars painted in lapis rose to painted ceilings. Torches burned with perfumed oil, and smoke curled like silk through the air. The marble beneath her slippers shone so brightly she could see the tremor in her own reflection. Servants flattened themselves against the walls with bowed heads as Esther walked by.

At last, Hegai stopped before a set of double doors. They were like her harem chambers, only grander, carved with scenes of conquest and roaring lions.

"This is where I must leave you," he said. His gaze held the weight of a thousand words.

Esther breathed deeply. This was it. Her hands trembled, and her palms were cold, but her mind was oddly at ease.

"Thank you, my dear friend," she said, bowing low to the ground. A shared understanding settled between them, an understanding that her gratitude was not simply for his guidance. It was for their camaraderie, for his kindness.

Hegai took her hand, returning the bow. "You have restored my hope that perhaps, one day, my home will return to greatness."

He pushed open the doors, and Esther walked in.

———

As a child, Mordecai had often praised Esther for her keen eye. She noticed everything, which made it difficult to hide things from her. At just five years, she would point out the slightest stain on his tunic, the bags under his eyes after a long day's work, the twinkle in his gaze after a horrendous joke. He always failed at surprising her on birthdays, for her awareness far surpassed his efforts to maintain secrecy. This had been at the center of many laughs over the years, but Esther hoped that whatever observational skills she had would come into use now.

The king's chambers were not so different from her own. A similarly lavish bed sat on the side, and a grand window overlooked the plush carpet of floral motifs. Her pulse electrified at the sight. A small table holding an array of dishes stood surrounded by cushions at the foot of the bed. King Xerxes was at the edge of the table, his eyes fixed on Esther as she walked in.

"Good evening, my lady," His voice was surprisingly gentle, though it rang with the hollowness of repetition.

"Good evening, my king."

Esther's heart pounded wildly. She forced her nerves to still as she studied the king, this figure who seemed more like a myth than a reality. He didn't look like a god, nor did he glow with any supernatural radiance. He was just…a man. Someone she might've encountered in the city's bazaars without a second glance. He had longer brown hair that fell in slight waves, the ends grazing the fabric of his off-white tunic. His beard was trimmed to the sharpness of Persian royalty. A militant edge cut through his gaze, though his eyes appeared softer now. More approachable.

One didn't need an observant eye to see that the king was weary. He hid it behind a smile, but Esther didn't miss the dark circles cupping his eyes or the clouds over his countenance. There was much on his mind. She could hardly believe the instruction she endured was to prepare her for one man, a man who appeared no less human than she did.

"Come," he said. "Let us eat."

Esther channeled her focus into keeping her hands still, lest she nervously begin fidgeting with them. The lessons of her training resounded more clearly in her mind than they ever had. She stilled her features into calm nobility, her eyebrows slightly arched and lips down. Her hands folded in front of her stomach as she moved forward. She lowered herself to the ground, stacking her knees atop each other to the side.

"What is your name, fair maiden?" he asked, his eyes never leaving her face. Words were harder to grasp under his intense gaze.

"They call me Esther, Great King."

"It's a pleasure to meet you," he said, gesturing to the food. "Eat as you wish."

They sat in silence as Esther commanded herself to take bites of fruit. Her stomach was tangled in one enormous knot of nerves. Any food going down her throat threatened to come back up again. She focused instead on the king, studying his full brows and the severe lines of his face.

What was she to make of him? He had the civility of a ruler, but his words felt like the lines of a script memorized against his will. He was an actor in a scene he did not wish to play. Esther couldn't discern if his exhaustion stemmed from the other maidens or the war. Perhaps a combination of the two.

"My king," Esther began, steadying her voice. She had learned the wisdom of silence, but she also knew the wisdom of compassion. "What troubles you?"

He looked up at her from his plate, more alert than he had appeared during their first exchange. "What gives you the impression that my mind is uneasy?"

"It is written all over your face," she replied, her lips curving into a small smile. "Tell me what grieves you."

The king looked at her differently now, almost inquisitively. She focused on maintaining the smile on her face, not straying her gaze away from his own.

It seemed she had opened the gates to a flood of afflictions. The kingdom's strife against Greece was tearing him apart. As his ships failed and more men fell to their spears, the legacy of his father ate at his conscience. He mentioned little about the maidens, which Esther was glad for. She wasn't just another girl in a sea of options—she was now a confidant in matters beyond her.

"I once thought my path was clear," the king continued, "but I've discovered that trail led only to a dead end."

Esther knew what it was to question her place in life, especially during her time in the harem. Was her role to serve her family or to be the queen of Persia? What was she training for? Kyra would never admit it, but Esther knew she had wrestled with the same thoughts. Kyra believed her purpose was to exact vengeance against her family. Yet she remained empty, even at the prospect of bringing her revenge to life.

"Perhaps it's time to assess your heart, my king," said Esther.

"I have scoured the depths of my mind for a purpose," he replied. "I have found temporary motivations, but they are just that. Fleeting."

"If I may be so bold, can I tell Your Majesty a story?" The words came out of her mouth before she could stop them.

He tilted his head, amused at the request. "Of course."

"There was once a king named Saul, the first of many rulers to lead his people," Esther began. As she spoke, she heard Mordecai's voice echoing beneath her own. She saw his face as it had appeared over countless Shabbat meals, a welcoming smile on his lips as he passed this very story down to her.

"He was chosen for his strength and stature, and all who saw him admired him. He was clever in judgment and careful in strategy." Her hands were no longer folded in front of her lap, moving animatedly as extensions of her mouth. "When disputes arose, King Saul resolved them quickly. He reasoned his way through battle when enemies knocked at the door. Under his rule, the kingdom grew secure, and his people praised him."

"A man fit for rule," the king interjected, smiling slightly.

"So it seemed," Esther continued. "But what sustained him at first did not sustain him in the end. There came a moment when Saul was given a charge that could not be reasoned around. A greater king, one who had elected Saul into royalty, ordered him to destroy an evil ruler named Agag. Saul was to annihilate the king and all of his people's possessions."

Xerxes shifted slightly.

"Saul obeyed this higher king in appearance," she said softly. "He wiped out King Agag's people, but he spared Agag himself, along with his valuable treasure. Saul spoke as if he had fulfilled his charge completely, but his intentions were dishonorable and selfish. Partial obedience is disobedience, and soon something in King Saul hollowed. He had disobeyed the greater king. Fear took root, followed by jealousy. He guarded his throne with a cruel kind of reason, one that blocked out all love and humility.

"When defeat finally arrived as his enemies closed in, Saul's strength failed, and he fell upon his own sword. Though he did not lack in intelligence or courage, he had lost the heart that once made him worthy to rule."

King Xerxes's expression morphed into discontent. "Kings are always judged more harshly in stories than they are in reality. Why would you regale me with such a depressing tale?"

"Because, my king," Esther began, "this ruler has a valuable lesson for us all. The heart and mind are two very different things. They work together in harmony, but they were not created to operate as one without the other. The mind is the center of reason, but the heart is the center of love." She looked at him intently. "King Saul, a man who won the world, died in discontent. His impressive life became meaningless without love, just as ours can."

Esther held her breath. King Xerxes was silent, his hands folded on the table in concentration. She had been taught that entertaining the king was a noble pursuit, but she hoped he didn't know her story belonged to the Jews. Though he may have been more tolerant of her people, tolerance did not mean absolute acceptance.

"You are a noble storyteller, and you ask noble questions," he said, finally breaking the silence. "And you have even nobler insights. Since the passing of my father and mother, I have had little reason to love."

"Take heart, Your Majesty," Esther smiled. "What you seek may be closer than you realize."

"And how do you propose I love?"

"Love never gives up. You must do the same, my king."

He nodded slightly, his brow no longer taut in anguish. He rose from the floor, extending his hand out. "Come, my lady." She weaved her fingers through his own. His hand was warm with life. She could feel the rhythm of his heart against her wrist, their pulses beating in tandem.

A strange groundedness had taken root in the air, and Esther let it carry her forward to the king's bed. It felt as though the world itself had stilled, holding its breath in quiet witness. The curtains whispered softly in the night breeze. The candlelight burned low, casting wavering halos on the walls.

That night, she yielded herself to all that was asked of her with a quiet fortitude, one she had not known she possessed. In all the months within the harem, she had imagined this moment as a storm, something to be endured, even survived. To her greatest shock, Esther's heart wasn't in turmoil. The tempest she had braced herself for had passed without striking. In its wake, the skies of her spirit opened. Conviction rooted in her heart, and her question was finally answered: *she knew what to do.*

Whether she walked with the weight of the crown on her temples or in the sandals of a subject, she would walk bearing the treasure of her people and her heritage.

14

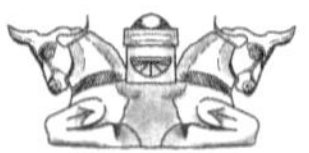

ER HOOD WAS TOO SMALL. Zelah pulled the dark robe over her head, quickening her steps. The frigid night air whistled past her, biting her nose and springing tears into her eyes. She wasn't supposed to be here. She didn't know how she would return to the harem, but none of that mattered. Zelah could find a way back later.

Her heart collapsed in relief as she came across the familiar adobe walls and flowered pots of her home. Zelah crawled through the front window and pressed an ear against her Māman's door. Nothing. Zelah sighed—she was probably spending the night at the brothel. She snaked through the familiar hall until the object of her greatest anguish came into sight. Her sleeping sister lay still on the bed, beads of sweat dotting her forehead. The room reeked with the foul acidity of vomit. Zelah controlled her breaths, feeling bile rise to her throat. She placed a hand on her sister's cheek. Her skin burned. She groaned in her slumber, the sound thick with illness.

"Everything will be alright soon, *khahar*." Zelah pressed a kiss to her forehead, her lips tingling from the damp heat. She took her hand, so cold in contrast. "Your pain will disappear. Just hold on. Just a little longer."

———

A leader feared by death itself. That had been the chant of the Persian armies after King Xerxes's victory at Thermopylae, the vein connecting Greece's upper and lower halves. The golden years of Xerxes's reign. The battle had sent several young Persians into early graves, but it had unleashed a greater bloodbath filled with the hearts of fallen Greeks. King Xerxes slaughtered hundreds of men single-handedly, the people said. He terrorized men with a single glance. They cowered at the sight of his blade. How strange. Esther studied the leader feared by death itself under the sheets beside her. Sunlight poured through the windows, casting a glow over his sleeping frame. She marveled at how vulnerable, how human, King Xerxes looked with his eyes closed. His body rose and fell with the waves of sleep. The serenity of his features smoothed the harsh lines of his cheeks and the space between his brows.

Shaashgaz, the eunuch of the second harem, ushered her out of the chamber before King Xerxes could rise. A silk covering enveloped Shaashgaz's head, his eyes warm in the light. She cast one final glance toward Xerxes before turning away, following the eunuch through the palace corridors into the second House of Women.

"I have heard much about you," Shaashgaz said, smiling at her. "Hegai has nothing but kind words for you."

"Hegai tends to exaggerate his good opinion of others," Esther replied, smiling. "I consider him a wonderful friend."

"His assessment of excellent character is sharp," the eunuch continued. "I'm sure his praise was not far from the truth."

Esther tilted her head politely with a smile. It seemed she was not the only one who cherished Hegai's character.

"You'll be escorted to your new quarters later," Shaashgaz spoke. "Your attendants from your previous chambers will serve you until all maidens have seen the king."

They arrived at a small wooden door, unlocked by the turn of a golden key. It opened to an expansive common room, its ambience made comfortable by sets of plush couches and plates of fruit on polished tables. Candles flickered on wooden stands, illuminating the space with a warm light. Maidens lounged on the couches, huddled in small groups. Her heart leaped as she noticed Kyra leaning against the corner of the wall. Zelah sat nearby in solitude, throwing a heated glance at Esther before turning away.

Esther lowered herself beside Kyra, relief and excitement tumbling out of their lips.

"I'm so glad you're here," Kyra grinned. "I've missed my Lady Sunshine."

"Likewise," Esther smiled, clutching her friend's hand. She considered asking her how her time with the king had been, but she decided against it. A vague inquiry was safer. "How have you been feeling?"

Esther had relied on her friend's love of conversation to uncover how her night with King Xerxes unfolded, and Kyra did not disappoint. They spoke in hushed tones to prevent the other maidens from overhearing, but that didn't stifle Kyra's animated gestures. She recounted everything that had transpired in the king's chambers—the meal they shared, the compliments he had lavished upon her. Listening, Esther couldn't help but wonder how much Kyra's lust for the crown had shaped her presentation before the king.

"It wasn't my first time serving him, but I doubt he remembered me," Kyra continued. "I've heard people in the streets condemn him. They complain loudly of his arrogance." Her tone took on a softer edge. "But I don't believe he is the monster everyone perceives him to be. And his military experience makes him wonderful in bed."

Esther slapped her arm playfully, but something felt off. Kyra often complained of servitude to Xerxes as the chains of her bondage. She seemed taken by him, but was it by his character or by his throne?

"There is always much more beyond the surface of a person," Esther replied. "I'm sure those complexities are tenfold when it comes to the rank and responsibilities of royalty."

"But how about you, Esther?" Kyra asked, popping a grape into her mouth. She plucked another for Esther. "How was your time with King Xerxes?"

Esther would have loved to divulge every detail of their conversation. It was thrilling, after all, to have spoken with the king. But some force held her back. Their exchange felt private. It was fragile, unfit for other ears. He had been vulnerable with her, and she did not want to risk turning his vulnerability into court gossip. She shared what she could, carefully skirting around the king's deeper confessions.

"You have a deep heart, Esther," Kyra said when she finished. "One that I'm sure any sensible man would be drawn to."

Esther smiled, assuring her friend that her beauty and boldness were forces of their own. What a strange dynamic this was. Kyra wanted the crown more than Esther ever had. It was bizarre to be praised for the king's affection by the very girl competing for it. Esther only hoped that whatever favor King Xerxes bestowed would not splinter the fragile thread of their friendship.

Day by day, more maidens were escorted into the second harem. The space had not been constructed for so many bodies at once, and it was growing crowded. When she wasn't in her chambers muttering Hebrew blessings, Esther retreated to the gardens, sitting on the grass under shaded trees in silence, but her thoughts were loud. King Xerxes often came to mind. She saw the surprising gentleness in his voice and the pain in his eyes. And, of course, Mordecai dwelled in her innermost thoughts.

"It seems we're both overwhelmed by the growing crowd."

Esther's head snapped up at the familiar, honeyed voice. Zelah lowered herself beside her, a sheer dress highlighting the curve of her chest. Her lips were upturned ever so slightly, but the blackness of her eyes made the smile hollow, even malicious. Esther's shoulders tensed.

"What a surprise, Zelah."

"You speak so elegantly, Esther," she smiled. "No wonder you flatter so nicely."

"Can I help you with anything?" Esther asked, plastering a smile on her face.

"I would like you to help me understand something," Zelah began. She plucked a blade of grass from the ground, tearing it neatly in half. "You keep to yourself."

Esther's gaze remained fixed on the trees ahead. "I enjoy solitude, especially in this crowded place."

Zelah hummed. "Indeed. I suppose that's why you speak to only a few of us."

Esther folded her hands tighter in her lap. "You seem fond of observing me."

The corners of Zelah's mouth curled upward. "I observe everyone—it's unwise not to." She released the torn grass from her fingertips. Esther watched as it fell limp to the ground. "Sometimes when I look at you, I feel as if I'm looking at one part of a much deeper whole."

Esther finally turned her head, irritation rising in her. "You think highly of your own insight."

"I place great weight in mysteries," Zelah corrected. "And you are full of them."

A tense silence stretched between them. Esther hoped Zelah couldn't hear the furious beating of her heart. Her face reeked with conceit, as if she knew something Esther didn't.

"This harem is growing crowded, Esther," said Zelah, sighing loudly. "That means there's room for only one of us."

"The king will choose as he pleases."

"Of course." Zelah rose, brushing the dirt from her robes. "But great rulers like him prefer women who are loyal, women rooted in who they are."

She turned then, an unsettling glint in her midnight gaze.

"By the way," she added casually. "You may want to close the door to your chambers next time."

15

AMAN GAZED AT HIS REFLECTION IN THE MIRROR. His slight beard cut across his chin at the sharpest angle, no strand out of place. He traced the scar marring his right cheek. The pad of his finger dipped into the groove of the old wound, now smoothed over by time. He turned to the golden trays of rings and chains beside the vanity. Haman slid the gems onto his hand, watching the faceted diamonds wink with each turn of his wrist. He gave his robe one last tug in satisfaction.

Chariots rattled over stone as he approached the palace complex. A eunuch swung the doors to the throne room open. Haman entered with an armful of scrolls, handing them to the nearest servant. The marble was cold against his fingertips as he lowered his head before Xerxes.

"Your Majesty, I deliver the court's monthly report."

King Xerxes nodded. "Well done, Haman."

"Is there anything else I can do for you, King Xerxes?"

"Alert the courts in every province that a new queen shall soon be crowned," the king said. Haman's eye latched onto the signet ring on Xerxes's finger, the metal glinting lustrously in the light. "The time to restore order has arrived."

"As you say, Great King."

The throne room doors shut behind Haman with a hollow thud. The palace gates yawned open to the city. Bigthan and Teresh stood watch at their posts, unmoving with spears in hand. Haman slowed as he passed, shooting a knowing glance at them. The men inclined their heads in silent understanding. Haman pulled his hood low over his face and slipped beyond the gates, walking away from the palace.

———

The grass murmured against her feet as Esther walked along the courtyard's winding path. The birds sang their morning melodies, and the trees rustled in greeting to one another. The flora had never appeared brighter, the fountains never purer. Esther breathed deeply, feeling new life rush through her spirits. With each exhale, she released another fragment of the image of Zelah that burned in her mind, released the knowing glint in her eyes and the angled curve of her lips.

"I thought I might find you here."

Esther's heart soared at the familiar deep voice. She turned, eyes alight with recognition.

"Hegai!" Esther forgot her composure entirely. She rushed forward and embraced him, burying her face briefly in the folds of his robe. He let out a soft breath of surprise before holding her close, wrapping his arms around her with a warmth that reminded her of Mordecai. "What are you doing here?" she asked.

"I'm here to escort you," he said. When Esther tilted her head in confusion, his voice softened, as if weighed down by the significance of his message. "The king requires your presence, Esther."

Esther's heart threatened to break out of her chest. King Xerxes? Surely he didn't intend to…

The temptation to probe tugged at her, but she kept her lips shut. She took Hegai's arm with an easy familiarity, a motion that had become instinctive.

Esther would never forget that journey to the king's throne room, palms clammy and pulse pounding in her neck. Her legs trembled at the uncertainty awaiting her. She held her head up high as the memory of walking to King Xerxes's chambers on that fateful night returned to her in flashes. She was reliving the adrenaline, the fear. Only this time, she didn't know what to expect.

The throne room was the most magnificent space. She entered the expanse beside Hegai, the eyes of the court latching onto her. The walls soared up to the heavens, supported by columns flanked by bull heads and carved coils. Sculpted paintings ran along the bottom edges of the room, depicting processions of people bowing before the king. Impossibly intricate markings danced across the ceiling, embellished by golden filigree.

King Xerxes sat in the aisle on a throne of rich velvet. He looked remarkably different from the time Esther had encountered him in his chambers. He had appeared more normal, more approachable in his sleeping gowns. Now he was god-like—unreachable and powerful. A cloak of deep blue cascaded down his shoulders, contrasting the gleaming crown on his temples. He held the royal golden scepter in his right hand, the top adorned with the head of a panther. The creature's sculpted eyes pierced straight through her own. A chill rushed down Esther's spine. Despite the splendor of her jade green gown, she suddenly felt underdressed. Esther mirrored Hegai as he bowed low before the throne, knees falling to the ground.

"Your Majesty, I present to you Esther of Susa."

"Rise, my faithful servant."

Esther watched carefully as Hegai addressed the king. Xerxes's expression softened in a way she hadn't seen before. His reply was quiet, almost conversational. They must've been closer than they let on. Hegai stepped away to the side of the chamber, leaving her exposed in the open space before the throne. Now Esther knelt before the king alone.

"Rise, Esther of Susa."

Esther rose to her feet. Months of training revealed itself in the straight lines of her shoulders, the slight downward tilt of her chin, the placement of her hands before her torso. Her night with the king had been intimate, but now there was no space for informality. She was standing in the throne room before the King of Kings.

"Great King." She bowed once more, delicately lifting the fabric of her skirt.

The king remained silent. His gaze lingered on her with an intensity that made her breath come in shorter bursts. Somewhere behind her, metal scraped softly against the polished floor as a guard adjusted his stance. Esther wondered with sudden clarity whether she had been summoned not to be elevated, but to be punished for some wrongdoing. Fear took hold of her heart as Zelah's knowing smirk flashed through her mind. *Had she discovered her secret and told the king?*

"Do you know why you stand here?" Xerxes said at last.

"I know only that I was commanded to come." Esther felt the eyes of the court settle on her, as if measuring whether she would falter. With a jolt in her chest, she noticed a group of maidens seated among the court nobles, maidens she had trained with in the harem. Kyra sat among them, her eyes pinning Esther with a crushing fierceness. *I want that crown, Kyra had said. I desire it more than anything in this world.* Esther averted her gaze.

King Xerxes rose from his throne. A sharp intake of breath rippled through the room. Esther's blood hummed in her ears, her breath hitching. This is where I die, Esther thought. I've wronged the king somehow, and now I'm paying the price. She braced herself for the boom of his voice declaring punishment, for the strike of his scepter against the ground in retribution.

Then Xerxes bowed before her.

"No longer shall I be addressed as your Great Ruler alone," he said, rising from the ground. "There will be another."

The court froze. He moved closer to Esther, the sound of his steps against the stone ringing louder than a trumpet.

King Xerxes extended his hand toward her. "And she stands before me."

Esther's breath caught as he took her hand. The warmth of his palm startled her, human and real and terrifying.

Her skin jumped. Every nerve in her body was alert, but she stilled her features into calmness.

"My queen," King Xerxes said quietly. His eyes never left hers as he pressed a kiss to her fingers. "Please accept my hand and this kingdom with it. Be my bride, and everything you desire shall be yours."

The world stilled around Esther. The trees and the creatures and the galaxies held their breath, leaning in to hear her response. His touch was electrifying. The word *queen* echoed in her ears, heavy with a promise and a burden. Esther thought of Mordecai, of her people she could not claim. Yet there she was, a Jew standing before the king of Persia. The King of Kings, a man who bowed to no one, kneeling before her in affection and anticipation.

Esther lifted her chin.

"I accept, my king."

16

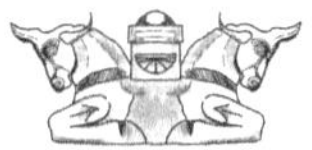

HE EYES OF MEN WERE WORLDS made with the wind and sand of the human soul. The eyes swirled with malice, with love, with hate, with anger, with compassion. In great sorrow, they overflowed with tears. In great anguish, they glistened with pain. In great rage, they darkened with seething shadows.

In the throne room, Kyra's eyes had blazed with all three.

Esther sat awake in her royal sheets, staring blankly at the ceiling paintings. Of all the beautiful features Kyra possessed, her eyes were the most distinct—speckles of hazel in an onyx abyss, a canvas of expression. Kyra's eyes had once looked at her with affection. Now they were haunting.

Esther could accept the animosity of the other maidens. Zelah had proven to her that malevolence was a robe worn more often than kindness. She could tolerate hostility from people who did not truly know her. But not Kyra. Just the thought of her friend's contempt made Esther's chest twist in aching knots. Competition for the king's favor had always loomed over their heads. Before, Kyra had laughed about it, joked that no man could dismantle their bond. What had changed? Esther was clinging to the rope of their friendship, but maybe the rope was just a threadbare string. Maybe it was time to let go.

The day of the coronation arrived. Esther assessed herself in the mirror, surrounded by her handmaidens. Her lips were painted with a pinkish powder. Kohl lifted the lines of her eyes, and her hair was woven into a crown of its own. She thought the gowns of the harem were extravagant, but they paled in comparison to the rich turquoise silk sighing over her skin. Emeralds and semiprecious stones gleamed in perfect rows. The neckline followed the shape of the golden chains adorning her chest. The dress clung to her torso and fell like elegant curtains, thinly veiled by a silk overthrow. Adara carefully placed the royal headdress on Esther's temples.

"Are you ready, Your Majesty?" Nava asked, smiling.

Esther cringed. "I'm not a queen yet."

"You will be in about ten minutes," Elina countered, laughing.

"She has always looked like a queen to me," Zarine added.

"Of course she has," Adara spoke. "You look beautiful, my lady."

Esther embraced her maidens, feeling a slight lump in her throat. "You'll come visit me, won't you?" she asked, half-jokingly.

"Of course." Adara waved them to the door. "There will be time to talk later, but we must be moving. Follow me, my lady."

Esther recognized the path they were taking, the path Hegai had taken her through to the throne room, where King Xerxes had declared his affection for her. They arrived outside the elaborate doors. Esther pressed her ear to the wood, taking in the lively noise of the crowd. Nerves shot through her chest. She clutched Adara's hand, squeezing it tightly.

"We must leave you now," Adara spoke gently. "I wish you luck, Queen Esther."

Esther watched as her handmaidens disappeared behind the corridor. She was alone. Only a door stood between her, the entire court, the king himself, and the crown that was to be put on her head.

The doors swung open. Esther's breath rang loudly in her ears. The lavender perfume on her neck wafted through her senses into the folds of her brain, chiding her nerves to relax.

Movement flickered at the edges of her vision as every head in the court snapped to her, but she saw only one man. King Xerxes sat on the throne, luminous in sweeping robes that mirrored hers. Though he was at the room's far end, his gaze burned through her as if she were right before him. A second throne stood beside him. Bejeweled stairs led to the empty seat. Every gold frame and glittering stone of the throne seemed to wink at her, beckoning her closer. *This seat is for you,* they whispered. *There's no going back.*

The king's voice thundered off the walls. "Announcing Esther of Susa."

A plush velvet carpet stretched across the floor before her. Heart shaking and legs trembling, she steadied her tremors into graceful steps. The voices of her instructors resounded through her mind. *Chin lifted, spine straight.* She felt the eyes of the crowd following her, a silent tide pressing against her down the length of the room. From the corner of her eye, she caught Hegai standing beside the king. He dipped his head slightly in encouragement.

King Xerxes began to speak. Something about her beauty, of the qualities he discerned in her, but his words blurred at the edges. Though his voice rang through the chamber, it sounded distant, as though Esther was suspended in time. The world narrowed to the space between her and the throne, the weight of the moment settling around her in air too thick to breathe.

"Rise, Esther of Susa."

King Xerxes reached for the crown beside him. He rose from the throne and removed Esther's headdress. Cool air hushed through her braids. She knelt before the king, the crown's cold metal sending a tingle down her spine. Esther took her place beside him as he enveloped his fingers over her shaking hands.

"Hail Queen Esther!" King Xerxes shouted.

"Hail Queen Esther!" The court echoed, rising from their seats.

The King of Kings returned to the throne beside his bride. The magi of the royal temple entered the space, dressed in the ceremonial wedding headdress. He unfurled the parchment in his hands.

"May the gods witness and bless this union," he spoke. "Let us begin."

———

Someone was shaking her. Leila opened her eyes blearily. She clutched her temple, grimacing at the pounding ache in her head. Shadi and Amir gazed down at her, brows furrowed in concern.

"How are you feeling, Leila?" Shadi placed a small white flower at her bedside. The petals were browning at the tips.

Leila let out a feeble groan, shifting under the sheets. Gods, her head hurt. "What are you guys doing here? You shouldn't come too close."

A light suddenly entered Amir's eyes. "We know, we know. But don't you hear it in the streets?"

Leila elevated herself to her elbows, looking out the window. "I hear nothing."

"Listen more closely."

Muffled shouting stirred in the distance. Leila strained to make out the words above her throbbing temples. The chant was growing louder and louder, closer and closer.

Hail Queen Esther!

Hail Queen Esther!

Esther. Elation soared through Leila's heart. Could it be? Was that why she had disappeared, why she hadn't come to visit her in her sickness? The words of the proclamation Leila had seen all those months ago flashed in her mind with a sudden clarity. King Xerxes had declared his quest for a new queen. And he had chosen one. *Queen Esther.*

Surely many women went by Esther in the empire. The chances were so slim. But as Leila looked to her friends for confirmation, there was no mistaking the beams on their faces.

"Do you think she would let us into the palace?" Shadi asked excitedly.

For the first time in months, Leila laughed. The searing in her chest flared, but it didn't matter. Excitement coursed through her like a powerful medicine.

"Hail Queen Esther," Amir said with a toothy grin.

Leila's smile mirrored his as she closed her eyes. "Hail Queen Esther." Her voice blended into the cries of the streets, now ringing as clear as the day.

Hail Queen Esther!

Hail Queen Esther!

——

There was no shortage of wine that night. Esther drank in the sight of the royal dining setting. A long mahogany table hosted a round of elaborate seats. Boisterous nobles reveled in their drunkenness before the elaborate feast, and the princes of the provinces bellowed in laughter to one another. She sat beside King Xerxes. Her practiced smile felt permanently plastered to her lips.

"My queen," Carshena spoke. One of Xerxes's advisors, Esther recalled. "You're a beautiful woman, eh? If I were king, I would throw an even grander feast for you."

Esther veiled her distaste. His words jumbled clumsily, his pupils under a haze. "Such kindness," she replied. "Though we must agree that His Majesty is unparalleled in the extravagance of his banquets."

Carshena waved flippantly, turning away to talk with the noble beside him. Esther shook her head.

"Is that man bothering you?"

Esther turned to a gently worn face, one that couldn't be much older than the king's. His eyes crinkled with good humor. A neatly trimmed beard outlined his chin, highlighting lifted cheekbones. He was quite handsome, save for the jagged scar cutting across his right cheek. The darkness of the wound was unsettling.

She put on a smile. "Your concern is appreciated, but we were simply having a friendly exchange. What do they call you, good sir?"

He ducked his head in a bow, his hand raised politely to his chest. "Haman, Your Majesty."

Esther smiled. "A pleasure, Haman. I hope you're enjoying the festivities."

"How could I not?" He raised his wine goblet. The stack of silver rings decorating his fingers glinted in the light. "There is great joy in celebrating greatness. You are the hallmark of this evening, my lady."

Esther raised her own goblet. "You have a way with words, Haman. I pray it treats you well."

"You're very gracious. Of course, only the gods can determine the course of my life."

"How insightful." She lifted the wine to her painted lips, concealing her smile as she felt the earthy taste run down her throat. There was something to this man, something she couldn't quite put her finger on. "I've accepted that the outcome of situations is largely out of my control," Esther continued. "We can only trust in purpose."

He laughed goodheartedly. "You have much wisdom, Your Majesty."

"Well, a queen does the best she can," Esther allowed a smile. Flattery was a funny thing. It was a glittering weapon, lovely to behold but seldom offered in innocence. Haman was presenting his entire arsenal.

He opened his mouth to say more, but King Xerxes rose with his wine goblet to the air, drawing the attention of all in the room. "Listen well," he began. "I proclaim this the feast of Esther to honor our new queen. Today is the first of many holidays to celebrate our union and the beginning of a prosperous era. To Queen Esther!"

"To Queen Esther!" the assembly echoed, lifting their goblets.

The king lowered himself beside Esther. "Are you enjoying this evening, my queen?"

Her cheekbones ached from smiling, but for her new husband, she could spare one more. Her lips turned upward. "It's lovely. Though if I may be so bold," she subtly gestured toward Haman, "who is that man?" He roared happily with a noble as they swung their goblets together.

Upon noticing Xerxes's gaze, Haman locked eyes with the king, acknowledging him with a small nod. "Ah, Haman," Xerxes began. "He is my highest court official and a diligent worker." The king brushed his bride's face lovingly. "But enough of other people. Are you content? Come to me with whatever you desire, and it shall be yours."

"You are most generous, my lord."

The king rose from his seat, taking hold of her hand. "Shall we retire for the night?"

Queen Esther bowed. "As you say, Your Majesty."

———

Haman stumbled along the nighttime streets of Susa. The air was quiet, a contrast to the morning flurry of the city. The feast had pulsed with music and laughter, yet once he marked the king and queen's absence, the merriment felt hollow. He was too tired to continue feigning interest in lesser men.

The wine had not lost its effect. His escort had left him only a short distance from home, but the path was blurry, and his cheeks were hot to the touch. Each step felt like its own long journey. Haman's heart jolted as he stumbled in the dirt, nearly tumbling to the ground. His face burned even darker as he turned to curse the object of his fall. An older man walked past him in a simple burlap sack, muttering under his breath. He recognized the coarse rise and fall of the Hebrew language. *A Jew.*

Haman spat at the man's feet, his blood boiling with fury. His words came out in a slurred brokenness. "Watch yourself, filth." What was a Jew doing so close to the palace? They had no place on these streets, let alone any streets in Persia. Xerxes could not allow this sickness to spread. The empire would always be restrained from true glory with such vermin roaming through its walls.

Rage overthrew intoxication in his mind. Haman threw his front door open, staggering to his bedchambers. His wife lay shrouded in shadows. A candle curled its tongue through the air on the nightstand beside her.

"My lord," Zeresh spoke softly and slowly, beckoning Haman towards her. She slid the robes off his shoulders. "What troubles you? I would think the king's festivities would invigorate you."

"Mark my words," Haman spoke as he inhaled her sickly sweet jasmine. Her scent entangled with the burning wax of the candle, and he felt his anger entangle with desire.

He smiled crookedly at the flicker in Zeresh's onyx eyes. "Any Jew who breathes the same air as me will feel the wrath of my people. They will wish themselves dead."

17

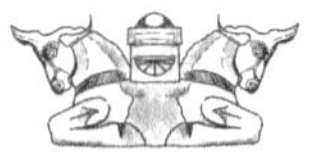

STHER HAD NOT SEEN THE KING IN FOUR WEEKS. You are only to see the king when he summons you, Hegai had said. Even the queen could not enter his presence unannounced. The King of Kings was set apart, a figure who belonged to the throne above any one person. Only when the royal golden scepter was extended could one enter without punishment. But no king had ever shown such mercy.

Four weeks were not long in the palace, but it was long enough for her memory to grow tender. In the rare quiet moments of her day, Esther replayed the sound of the king's voice, a voice that became unexpectedly gentle when they were alone. She saw his gaze soften as though she was not merely his queen but his beloved. She remembered the warmth of his hand around her own. She hadn't realized how deeply she anticipated those moments, the rare ease in his presence.

Esther ran her fingers along the inlaid gems of the throne's armrest. There must have been thousands of tiny stones on the surface. Each one glinted individually in a sea of color. A part of her still wondered whether she would ever grow accustomed to this life of immeasurable luxury. It was strange to have servants bow as she passed. Strange for every step to be weighed down by priceless silks. Strange to look in the mirror and see perfectly powdered features. She was comfortable, more than comfortable. Yet comfort did little to quiet the ache of absence.

Kyra had once told her that the human heart yearns for the familiar, that we come to love what we know. We are creatures averse to change, she had said, even when that change is good. Perhaps that was why Esther sometimes missed the cool hardness of the floor she once slept upon, or the small window she had gazed through each night, listening to the steady rise and fall of Mordecai's breaths.

Still, her longing did not negate duty. As Mordecai often told her, humans were created for greatness, not mediocrity. She would not settle for anything less than excellence. Of course, many of her obligations were not a particular source of joy. No sensible person jumped at the notion of sitting through long council meetings or conversing with snooty nobles.

But there was one duty Esther never found wearisome. On certain mornings, a steward would burst through her chambers with a sealed request—urgent, he would say—and she would immediately follow him to the throne room. Petitioners were admitted sparingly, and usually only when desperation pressed hard enough to reach the palace gates.

The people swept into the throne room with tears and bowed heads and trembling shoulders. A mother with a fevered child, or a farmer ruined by blight. A widow entrenched in debt, or a young family in destitution. She listened as they struggled to lift their eyes to meet hers. She called for physicians, and grains were distributed into homes at her command. Scribes strode through the cities armed with decrees bearing her seal.

The quiet of the throne room shattered as the doors burst open. Disbelief surged through Esther as Zelah sauntered into the chamber, her familiar black curls like a curtain of night. Even more shocking was her gaunt exhaustion, so far from the razor-like perfection Esther was accustomed to. Dark circles bordered her bloodshot eyes, and her steps dragged with invisible weights. Esther realized she had never seen Zelah without makeup. She seemed more human somehow.

The eunuch at her side bowed low. "Queen Esther, I present Zelah of Susa."

Zelah mirrored his posture. "Thank you for sacrificing your time, Your Majesty."

Esther politely dipped her head. Something in her shifted uncomfortably. In the House of Women, Zelah's glare on her had never eased. Their last interaction in the courtyard made both Zelah's hatred and suspicion crystal clear. Zelah knew Esther was not what she seemed. She might not have known of her Jewish heritage, but she knew something was amiss. What had she said? *Sometimes when I look at you, I feel as if I'm looking at one part of a much deeper whole.* And now Zelah kissed the ground before her feet. Her humility felt distant from the girl Esther knew. *Humans were averse to change.*

"Rise. What is your business, Zelah?"

"Queen Esther, my sister has fallen deathly ill." Her voice cracked. "May I be so bold as to touch your robe for the gods' blessing?"

Esther remained motionless. No one could enter the royal chamber bearing unauthorized weapons, and Zelah stood empty-handed. Whatever threat she posed, it would not be an attempt on her life. Esther inclined her head. "Come forward."

Zelah approached and knelt, fingers reaching for the hem of Esther's robes. The air between them felt strangely charged, like a small rock poised to trigger a catastrophic landslide. Then Zelah's grip tightened, just subtly enough to avoid the guards' attention. But enough for her knuckles to whiten against the turquoise fabric.

Zelah's head remained bowed. Her lips barely moved.

"I know your secret," she whispered with a dagger's edge. "You filthy, *Jewish* rat."

The heat drained from Esther's limbs, leaving a cold that settled deep in her bones. She *did* know. And worse, she was not afraid to speak it.

"The kingdom will riot if they find out," she continued, her voice taking on a manic edge. "You want to keep your secret, don't you? So you're going to listen to me. You're going to gather your best medics to cure my dying sister, and you'll give a portion of the king's gold to my family."

At Esther's command, the guards swarmed Zelah and pulled her away from the throne. Esther's features hardened as she looked down at her, someone she had once been so fearful of. Zelah had been reduced to a creature of sorrow.

"You were never supposed to be queen," she cried violently. "What witchcraft did you use on the king?" Zelah thrashed against the grip of the guards, arms and legs flailing in a ferocious, futile struggle.

"Your Majesty, we shall carry her away at once."

Esther held out her hand. "One moment. Zelah, what is your sister's name?"

Zelah looked up, tears forming rivers down her cheeks. "What's the point? Besides, you already know her."

The guard jostled her by the arm. "You will answer the queen."

"Leila. Her name is Leila."

Esther's heart dropped as understanding dawned upon her. There were hundreds of girls named Leila across the empire. But as Zelah lifted her eyes, recognition struck Esther in a wave. No wonder she had looked so familiar when they first met—the cheekbones, the shape of the mouth, the same defiant set of the chin. It was all the same. Though Zelah's brows were thinner and her nose sat higher on her face, the resemblance was undeniable. Leila, the mischievous girl who darted between market stalls, who tugged at Esther's sleeves and laughed care-freely.

Esther's fingers curled around the carved armrests of her throne. The pointed edges of the jewels bit into her palms. How had she never noticed? But Leila had never spoken of a sister.

"I saw you," Zelah hissed. "I saw you in the marketplace. The way she followed you." Her lip curled. "You stole my sister from me. She poured herself into you, loved you more than her own family. I care about her more than you ever have. And now she's wasting away, sleeping in her own vomit."

Esther's heart shattered. Against the shadows of sickness was the cruel contrast of Leila's bright grin and the reckless joy in her eyes. Leila lost her delight to nothing, but it seemed she had found a formidable opponent in her ailment. For a moment, Esther forgot the danger. Forgot the secret Zelah threatened her with. Leila was ill, and she hadn't known.

"Look at you," Zelah laughed hysterically. "Queen Esther, sitting on a throne worth more than my entire family's earnings. How does it feel to eat and drink gold, Your Highness?"

"Enough." Esther's voice echoed throughout the room. Her gaze fell upon the girl before her, on the remnants of tears staining her cheeks. She tried to remember all the hostility Zelah had shown her in the harem, but all she could see was Leila's face.

"Leila is a sister to me," she began. "That means you also are my sister, Zelah. I will do as you say. Leila will soon be restored to health."

Esther lifted her hand. The guards moved at once, turning Zelah away before she could respond. Esther watched solemnly as she disappeared through the gates, dark curls streaming down her back in the same unruly cascade she had once seen bouncing through the marketplace.

<hr>

The morning was young. Sunlight slipped through a window, pooling at the edge of a narrow bed. A girl who had not stood in weeks pushed herself upright. Her sister appeared before she could stumble, arms wrapped around her with relieved desperation.

On the bedside sat a woven basket. The honey cakes inside filled the room with the faint smell of flour. The girl studied them and smiled. She recognized the neat arrangement, the familiar aroma.

Across the city in chambers lined with marble and gold, the Queen of Persia brushed the last traces of sugar from her hair.

<hr>

One name was uttered in every corner of the city. Queen Esther. The title carried like wind through reeds. Mordecai heard it murmured beneath the awnings of the bazaar, in passing conversation, in court rumors. Everywhere he turned, there she was.

Queen Esther did not carry herself as a queen in his memory. She carried baskets too large for her arms and argued over the price of figs. She laughed too loudly and forgot to braid her hair properly. She cooked their evening meals and joked freely. No, Hadassah did not have the regality of Queen Esther. But in Mordecai's heart, there was no difference between them.

Age had made him softer than he cared to admit. In his younger years, Mordecai had been content to wait, to trust that time and providence would unfold as they must. Now patience thinned with each passing day. He found himself pausing outside his own doorway, listening to the quiet inside as though expecting Esther's voice to answer.

The house was smaller without her. He ate alone. Returned home in silence. His nights had become dreadful eternities as he stared at the ceiling. His thoughts circled endlessly, unceasingly returning to the same place of her loneliness, of her imprisonment. Was she well? Did she think of him as often as he thought of her?

Mordecai couldn't bear another day of solitude. He needed to see his daughter, to have proof of her safety. He had slipped into the palace grounds before, but the number of guards had doubled. Unfamiliar faces now stood at every entrance, and Hegai wouldn't be there to help him through.

Still, there was no harm in trying. Maybe she was lingering by the palace gates, Mordecai thought to himself as he trekked to the heart of Susa. His feet carried him with the memory of his midnight journeys to the House of Women, where Esther had once resided. The sun was just beginning to peak out above the horizon, casting a warm glow over Xerxes's empire. Mordecai delighted in this time of day, when life stirred in quiet blooms.

The morning air was sharp in his lungs. Mordecai's eyes traced the soaring columns as the palace facade came into view. Marble stairs led to the gates separating the palace from the rest of the city. Two hefty guards flanked either end, their copper skin glinting in the morning light. Mordecai sighed. He lowered himself onto a nearby bench, the concrete warm against his legs. He cradled his head in his hands. Why had he even bothered to come? Esther's duty to her people triumphed over all other priorities, including him. He could request an audience with her, but there was no telling when his petition would be processed.

Mordecai stood up to make the trek back home, remorseful over a wasted journey. Before he could take a step, a biting slap cut through the air. He froze.

Mordecai lowered himself behind the stone bench. The two men now stood inches apart. An angry welt sweltered on the cheek of one guard, as red as the silk ties of his armor. He clenched a trembling fist at his side as the other glared menacingly.

"You were not paid to back out of this deal like a coward, Bigthan," he seethed. "Remember why we are doing this."

Mordecai's foot crunched against gravel. It was loud, much too loud. A jolt electrified his heart. Mordecai's attention whipped back to the guards, but he quickly breathed a sigh of relief. They hadn't noticed him.

"We both understand Xerxes is not fit to rule," the guard continued. "Consider our gain. No longer will we stand out here like dogs—we'll be *kings*."

"Teresh, you waste your breath. I fully understand." Bigthan rubbed the lump on his cheek in contempt. "I trust that you have taken care of your end."

"I have the scrolls." Teresh patted the satchel dangling off his belt. "Tomorrow night, we enter the king's chamber when he's drunk as a donkey." They snickered. "Once we're done with him, he shall be king no longer. May the gods bless us."

They returned to their original positions like two loyal protectors of the crown, not two men lusting after murder. Every inch of Mordecai's skin felt too hot. Beads of sweat formed at his temples. Now he had no choice but to request an audience with Esther. He had to see her, not for his sake, but for the sake of the empire.

Or King Xerxes would be dead in hours.

Haman lounged in plush satin sheets. He twisted the ring on his index finger, an obsidian fragment carved into a serpentine coil. Zeresh hummed quietly beside him as he stroked her hair. The curve of her thigh rested tauntingly against his leg.

"How can you trust two palace guards with such an enormous responsibility?" said Zeresh. She twirled a wine goblet in her hand. "You paid no small sum for those parchments."

"I place my faith not in their character but in their appetite for gold. Trust me, my love." Haman planted a kiss on her temple. "They will not fail."

18

THE THRONE ROOM WAS DESIGNED TO GREET THE MORNING. When the sun climbed over the city walls, light beamed through the gilded windows in perfect streams. The dappled radiance hung in the air as if stuck in time. The glow beckoned the divine, and the warmth soothed like a loving caress.

Mordecai stepped into the throne room, a silhouette outlined in gold. His relaxed walk was unmistakable even from a distance. The light followed him as he moved forward, silvering the strands in his beard and brightening his eyes.

Esther's breath caught in her throat. He came to the foot of the dais and bowed lower than any noble she had encountered, his knees to the stone and forehead pressed to the ground. "Your Majesty."

Inclining her head, she folded her hands on her lap. She hadn't seen her Abba in months, not since Hegai had arranged their reunion at the harem. Esther's emotions welled in her throat all at once. The back of her eyes stung with tears as overwhelming relief threatened to break through. She stole sideways glances at the eunuchs beside her. No, she couldn't do this now. Esther stoned her features into stillness.

"What is your petition, sir?" she asked.

Mordecai looked up, locking eyes with her. "I wish to speak with my daughter, Queen Esther."

Esther motioned to the guard beside her. "Arman, please shut the doors. And clear everyone out. I'd like to speak to this man alone."

"Of course, Your Highness."

Their footsteps soon faded into the corridor. Esther burst from the throne, collapsing into Mordecai's familiar embrace. He grunted at the impact, then chuckled softly. Tears gathered at the corners of her eyes. She felt Mordecai's shoulders tremble with quiet sobs under her arms. He smelled of *chamin,* of earthy lentils and simmered cumin. The scent of home flooded her senses.

"You look beautiful, my Esther," Mordecai finally breathed. "I have missed you terribly."

Esther swiped her tears with a laugh. "Missed me or missed my cooking?"

"Your cooking."

Esther rolled her eyes. Mordecai laughed, a sound she hadn't heard for eons. The ache of his absence was healing with each smile, each twinkle in his eyes. "What are you doing here?" she said. "Is everything alright?"

His countenance shifted gravely. "I don't want to taint our short time together, Esther, but there's something you must know." His voice lowered to a whisper. "King Xerxes is in danger."

A sharp current ran through her. "What makes you so certain?" Threats were not uncommon in the royal court. It could be nothing more than the careless words of a drunken noble.

"I took a journey to the palace and overheard two guards plotting to kill the king tomorrow night." Mordecai took her hands in his. "I came as soon as I heard. If I believed it was said in jest, I wouldn't have bothered to beg for an audience with you. But their anger was real. And dangerous. You must be careful, Esther."

"What were their posts?"

"The central gates. One was named Bigthan, and the other Teresh."

Esther's heart lurched with fear. The prospect of two men deceitfully protecting a crown they sought to eliminate sent a chill down her spine. Not all servants of the king could be trusted. Some clutched daggers behind their backs, waiting to strike. Still, betrayal prowled much closer than she had thought.

Her chest twisted in discomfort. If these guards truly intended to murder the king, who else could be pledging false loyalty right under her nose?

———

Haman twisted the signet ring on his middle finger. An ornate table stretched between him and King Xerxes, flanked by the princes of Media. He kneeled on a plush cushion, his crimson robes pooling on the surrounding floor. Haman glanced at the jewels anointing the king's hand. The emerald and sapphire glinted in the low light as Xerxes gripped his golden scepter.

"Haman," Xerxes began, the corners of his eyes crinkling in a slight smile. "I'm impressed by your contributions to my empire. Someone of your competence must understand the challenges of ruling a great people. Trust is a scarce commodity."

"Of course, Your Majesty."

"However, it is a commodity I will extend to you." Xerxes extended his golden scepter over the table. "From this day forth, as my second-in-command, you shall reign over the princes and all else under my authority. Do you accept this honor, Haman?"

Haman bowed deeply, his palms pressing against the cool floor. "I accept, Great King."

Xerxes rose from the floor, thudding his scepter against the ground. "Hear me. All who enter the presence of Haman shall bow before him. To honor him is to honor me, your High King. Rise, my loyal chief."

Haman's pulse quickened as he stood. The princes and guards sank their heads before him. He drank in the sight of the nobility at his feet. "You are most gracious, my lord." His lip curled upward. "I swear to you that nothing shall mar our domain."

Xerxes hoisted his wine goblet to the sky. "To the gods and the greater good."

Haman lifted his goblet. A drop of wine escaped from the lip. It slid along the cup's golden engravings, trickling down Haman's forearm like blood. He swiped it off with a flick of his finger. "To the greater good."

———

Esther reclined on the luscious cushions, sinking into the velvet as she closed her eyes. A cool breeze whispered around her. Her open bedchamber windows exposed a sliver of twilight. The sun hung low in the sky, washing the world in a musky blue.

Adara swept into the room with a rolled parchment in her hands. She placed it in Esther's hands with practiced familiarity. "From His Majesty."

Esther smiled at her. After her coronation, she had made only one personal request—that the maidens who had tended her in the harem remain in her service, Adara most of all. There was no need for instruction between them now. By the week's end, Adara knew to arrange Shabbat ingredients in her chambers quietly. On those evenings, she kept the corridors undisturbed. Each morning, powders and brushes appeared at Esther's vanity before the sun fully rose. Adara selected her gowns with precise care, and Esther's jewelry never lay out of place. Trust was scarce, but not with Adara.

Esther turned the parchment over in her hands, scrunching her brows together. The king had not called for her in weeks, and her duties for the day had been fulfilled. Had she missed something?

She unraveled the parchment, met with elegant penmanship:

My Queen,

Esther rolled the parchment, unable to contain her rising smile. She rose from the cushions, smoothing the folds of her dress. "Care to walk with me, Adara?"

"Of course, my lady."

It did not take long for them to find King Xerxes. He sat on a stone bench at the foot of the fountain. The waters rippled quietly in the night. His simple white garments were so different from royal gossamer and gems. His hair fell freely around his shoulders, and the usual harshness of his gaze had softened. Esther dismissed Adara with a smile. She took the king's outstretched hand. Warmth blossomed in her cheeks at the familiar fit of their interlocking fingers.

King Xerxes brushed his lips against her hand. "It's lovely to see you, Queen Esther."

She bowed, and she found her smile was genuine. "Likewise, my king."

Darkness descended over the land, making way for glittering stars. The king and queen walked along the stone pathways of the garden, their steps steady and synchronized. The words were on the tip of her tongue. *Someone is going to kill you, King Xerxes. We must act now.* But the warning was caught in her throat. The serenity between them was rare, sacred. Something that couldn't be disturbed just yet.

"Queen Esther," Xerxes spoke. He turned toward a flowering vine, plucking the blossom. He placed the petals in her open palm and enveloped his fingers around her hand, concealing the flower. "Of all the beauties of this garden, what is your favorite to behold?"

Esther blinked in surprise. She remembered Hegai asking the same question during her first days in the harem. "Well," she hummed. "I have always adored myrtles. They seem like very joyful flowers. The way their petals reach forward and curl out makes it seem like they're in want of a hug."

The king laughed, the deep sound resonating in her temples. "Come," he said, holding out his arm. "I'd like to show you something, Esther."

She placed her hand gently on his forearm. Esther. Not Queen Esther. She smiled. He led her along a narrow stone path, their steps hushed in the night. The florets were motionless in slumber. Trees arched overhead in a canopy of branches, weaving through the starlight. They approached a towering wall of bushes sprinkled with pale pink and white buds. Xerxes parted the leaves, holding them back as Esther stepped through. She gasped.

The hedge had concealed an entire world. Torches hoisted on pillars cast an amber glow across the courtyard, illuminating the edges of leaves and stones. A clear pond lay at the center with the moon stretched across its surface, scattering shards of light. White myrtles formed a ring around the water. Their fragrance rose in the air, soft and pure. A dark tree hovered protectively overhead, its leaves rustling against each other. Lilies drifted in slow circles across the expanse.

"It's beautiful," she breathed. Esther knelt at the pond's edge, her fingers skimming the cool surface. Xerxes watched her with a slight smile. He reached into the water for a myrtle, holding it up to the torchlight. Esther gazed in delight as the petals glowed under the bronze flame.

In the garden, the palace didn't exist. The throne became a figment of her imagination, and court politics became a memory. Time loosened its grip. All Esther knew was the quiet rhythm of the water and the warmth of King Xerxes beside her. But even in the garden's stillness, Mordecai's words pressed at the edges of her thoughts. *King Xerxes is in danger.*

By the time they returned to the fountain, Esther knew she could no longer wait. She drew in a steady breath. "My king, I must tell you something urgent."

Esther observed his face as she spoke. It was deliberately calm, devoid of emotion. She wondered what he was truly thinking, whether he feared for his life.

When Esther finished, he nodded his head solemnly. "The matter shall be investigated at once. Who informed you of the plot?"

"Mordecai the Jew."

King Xerxes released a deep sigh. "It seems the Greeks are not the only ones out for my blood."

Esther smiled lightly. "All you need is one trustworthy man, King Xerxes. One loyal companion is worth more than ten thousand false ones."

A calm silence settled between them. She lowered herself into a deep bow. "Thank you for tonight, Your Highness. I had the most wonderful time."

Xerxes pressed one last kiss to her hand. "For you, my queen, anything."

19

**AMAN WAS A GOD.** With each step he took, another bowed. Man or woman, child or elder, noble or peasant, servant or master. It didn't matter. All lowered their heads before him. All conversation ceased in reverence. Power coursed through his veins, and for the first time in his life, he felt he had seized his wildest dreams. He was untouchable.

The gods seemed to smile favorably upon him. It was a brilliant day, the heat of the sun countered by a slight breeze. He smiled to himself as he rode atop a camel, accompanied by palace guards. Haman had an appointment with an eastern merchant, a crucial connection to keep the kingdom's wineries flowing. Given the king's affection for wine—even by royal standards, he snickered to himself—Haman couldn't afford any blunders.

Fortunately, his spirits were high. As they ventured farther out of Susa and into the Jewish province, Haman's lip curled into a sneer. He kept his gaze deliberately forward, swelling with glory as he saw the Jews stooping before him in his periphery. He smiled. The people who slew his forefathers were humbling themselves before an Agagite. How ironic.

Haman paused. He turned to his right, where an older Jewish man stood with his chest out. His gaze pierced directly through Haman. He certainly wasn't from wealth. Disgust unfurled in Haman's chest at the man's unkempt beard and dirtied robes. A rush of unadulterated rage consumed him in a flood, washing over his senses with a mighty roar.

"Jew." Haman spat at his feet, silently seething. He looked down at the man, keeping his voice level. "Will you not bow before your superior?"

"I only bow before those worthy of praise. You, sir, certainly are not."

"What is your name?"

The surrounding people shifted nervously, their heads still cast to the dirt. Some tried forcing him to the ground, but he waved their hands aside. "I am Mordecai, son of the tribe of Benjamin."

The palace guards beside Haman wielded their spears menacingly. "Bow before your Supreme Chief, as is instructed in the law."

Mordecai fixed his gaze on Haman. "I shall not."

The Agagite's anger exploded in flames of fury. In one sudden motion, the guards brought Mordecai to the ground, thrusting the hilts of their spears into his side. The old man clutched his ribs delicately. He sputtered, but never once did his eyes stray from Haman's face. Though Haman would never admit it aloud, there was an unnatural defiance in Mordecai's eyes. It was as if he didn't just see Haman, but saw *through* him.

Haman bit his tongue as his chest churned with wrath. He spat again, this time at Mordecai's face.

"Let this be a lesson to you all." Haman's voice boomed in the streets, and he relished the terror in the faces below. He guzzled the sight of mothers holding children behind their backs. "You will bow before your Supreme Chief, or you will hang from the king's gallows forever."

Haman gestured for the guards to press forward. He sat with his head held high, but he could still feel Mordecai's eyes burning into his back as he rode farther away.

———

Revenge was a fire. Left unchecked, revenge spread and swallowed all surrounding it, a storm of thick smoke and blazing flares. Time fueled its violence, and Haman basked in the heat. He had not forgotten his name. *Mordecai the Jew.* Ever since his defiance, Haman had thrown himself fully into the fire. The flaming tongues lapped at every surface of his body until he was a changed man. He had burned his old passivity, reviving as a man of change, a man of unswerving action.

Seasons passed, and so did life at the court. Haman bowed before King Xerxes and Queen Esther, flashing his teeth in winning smiles. With every glance at the king, he was reminded of the failure of his plot. It had not taken long for Bigthan and Teresh to be stripped of their titles and sent to rot in the dungeons. To his chagrin, he still hadn't uncovered the one responsible for exposing his accomplices.

"Haman, we must investigate each member of the court," Xerxes had said. "This attempt on my life cannot happen again."

"Thank the gods you were alerted to the development, Great King," Haman replied. "I had been investigating the matter myself, and how fortunate that my suspicions were confirmed. Praise be to your safety, King Xerxes." His words had been a dagger dipped in honey, a charming smile dripping on the surface of a seething heart.

Haman sat rigidly in his quarters. He turned over the stones in his palm, each marked with a tally—one for the month, one for the day. They felt cold in his palm, heavy with the weight of what the gods would decide. Haman closed his eyes, breathing in the incense curling beside him. He turned the stones in his hand one last time before tossing them, watching as they flipped through the air. The lots fell to the ground in subsequent *clinks*. Thirteen marks. Twelve marks. *The thirteenth day of the twelfth month.* The month of Adar, just eleven cycles away. Haman's face twisted into a smile.

He strode to the entrance of the court's central meeting chamber. A eunuch rounded the corner, lowering his head in a deep bow. "The king will see you now, Great Haman."

King Xerxes was tired. He sat erect in the council chair, but darkness shadowed his under eyes. His skin was sallow, and his grip on the golden scepter was looser. Haman stooped before him. The words flowed seamlessly from his lips, words he had crafted to perfection over weeks and weeks.

"Great King, there lives a group of people in your empire who think themselves above your laws. The Israelites live by the regulations of their own depraved culture. It is not in Your Majesty's interest to tolerate such wickedness." The memory of Mordecai's defiance burned through Haman's mind with striking clarity. He saw his feet planted to the ground, refusing to bow. "If it is pleasing to my lord, order the destruction of these people throughout the kingdom. I will offer ten thousand talents of silver to the men who carry out the order. I come as your humble servant, King Xerxes. Allow me to serve your people with divine justice.”

“The Israelites are guests in my domain,” said King Xerxes. “To honor your request would make us poor hosts.”

“Guests ought to respect their masters for extending such generosity. The Israelites have failed to do so.”

For a moment, Xerxes was silent. He removed the golden signet ring from his hand and slid it through Haman’s finger. The metal was cool against his skin. His pulse leapt at the sight of the king’s seal on his body, the ultimate insignia of authority.

“The silver is yours. Do with the people as you please,” King Xerxes finally broke the silence. “Seal the decree with my ring, and I shall have my couriers send the message to every province. You have my trust, Haman.”

“Of course, Your Majesty. Let us celebrate with a drink.” Haman ushered over a servant. He handed a wine goblet to the king before taking one of his own, thrusting it to the air. “Today marks the beginning of restoration. To Your Majesty, the empire, and our people.”

Xerxes mirrored Haman’s motion. “To the empire and our people.”

The two men drank heartily, their careless laughs growing louder with each swig of wine. Outside the palace walls, throngs of people clustered together to read the new decree.

> *By royal proclamation, subjects of this kingdom are alerted to a command of King Xerxes and your Supreme Chief Haman. A hateful people from the land of Israel, the people of Mordecai the Jew, live according to inferior ways above the desires of the High King. On the thirteenth day of the twelfth month of Adar, these Jews are to be utterly destroyed, young and old, men and women. Their possessions shall be seized as plunder, and no one will be spared. The people of King Xerxes will prepare themselves for this day according to His Majesty's divine command.*

The drunken howls of King Xerxes and Haman rose alongside the cries of the Israelites. A sinister choir filled the air, joining uncertainty with fear and bloodshed with inevitability.

20

OR THE FIRST TIME THAT
YEAR, the sun was not out. Clouds
brewed in the sky, somber and
impossible to ignore. A deep
darkness hovered over the Persian
Empire.

In the middle of the bazaar, Mordecai fell to his knees. Many passed by. Some shared his sorrow, others did not. His body heaved with thundering sobs. He rocked back and forth, fisting his tunic and tearing the fabric at the seams. The rough sand of the ground lacerated the skin of his knees, though he hardly felt the sting. Drops of blood stained the dirt beneath him. He had done this. How could he have forsaken his people? A searing pain ripped through his eyes, burning with the acid of his tears.

Mordecai rose from the dirt, walking aimlessly around Susa. Similar moans of anguish resounded in his ears as he passed by Israelite homes and swarms of Jews gathering around the decree. Different people, different families united in their lowered heads and trembling bodies. Their sounds of mourning blended with his own in a haunting chorus.

His people, the people of Israel, were going to perish.

And their deaths were on his shoulders.

21

STRING OF LAUGHTER LEFT ESTHER'S LIPS.** She sat at a polished mahogany table beside the princesses of India. Her spirits bubbled as stories overlapped and jeweled hands rose animatedly in the air. Diplomatic meetings were usually dreadful occasions. Snobby princes and haughty nobles puffed their chests unceasingly, and her forced smiles bruised the apples of her cheeks. But the princesses were remarkably pleasant. Trade negotiations had quickly dissolved into merriment as they laughed behind their wine goblets.

It was astonishing how quickly the atmosphere could change.

The chamber doors opened without ceremony. Her maidens swept into the room with seven of the king's eunuchs close behind. Their faces were grave, solemn with the sobriety borne of tragedy. Adara pressed her lips against the queen's ear, whispers heavy with distress.

The blood drained from Esther's face. Her fingers tightened against the edge of the table. For a fleeting second, her tears threatened to break through her composure. She pressed her palm to her mouth. Not here. Not in front of guests.

She inhaled once, steadying herself. "Please escort these lovely ladies to their chambers," Esther said gently to two of her maidens.

"Is everything alright, Your Majesty?" one princess asked.

"It soon will be." It took everything to keep her voice from breaking.

The door shut behind them. Esther brought her hands to her face. Her body wracked with quiet agony; despair streamed down her cheeks in rivers. The tears trailed down her jaw and fell to the floor. Her maidens and eunuchs stepped back, their heads bowed at the sight of their brokenhearted queen.

Esther could almost hear the Israelites' cries in her mind, their wailing joining with her own song of sorrow. *The people of Mordecai.* That was how the Israelites were addressed. Somewhere in the back of her mind, she wondered why, of all the Jews in the land, her Abba was the target of this looming massacre. And if Adara's words rang true, Mordecai was currently wandering in the city with tattered robes and bloodshot eyes.

Esther breathed deeply, settling her features into a careful mask of calm. Across the chamber, she met Hegai's eyes among the eunuchs standing before her. His gaze blazed with an intensity that almost startled her. Hegai was a man of stone. He betrayed no feeling. But now his eyes pierced through her with amazement, with shock, with curiosity.

Then it struck her. The decree exposed Mordecai's Israelite descent. Hegai had known him to be her guardian since the harem. He knew she was Jewish. To her disbelief, of all the emotions flickering in his eyes, one shone brighter than the rest: compassion.

"Hegai," she called. He knelt before her. "Get sheets of sackcloth and give them to Mordecai. He should be in the city square."

"Right away, Your Majesty."

Once Hegai stepped out of the door along with the other eunuchs, Esther sank to the ground. She clutched the hands of her maidens, her heart hammering in her chest. It felt like an eternity had passed before Hegai returned. To her confusion, the sackcloth remained in his hand.

"He refused to take it, Queen Esther," Hegai explained. "I insisted it was upon your orders, but he refused to accept it."

She shook her head. Even in mourning, Mordecai remained ever stubborn. "Return to him, Hegai, and ask how all of this came to be."

When he returned, each word that tumbled out of his mouth was a blow to Esther's chest—Mordecai humiliated after refusing to bow to Haman, the ten thousand talents of silver promised to those who murdered her people, the cruelty of the edict. She pored over a copy of the decree, the papyrus hot under her skin. The elegant penmanship was a brutal joke.

"Your Highness, there's one more thing," Hegai spoke, breaking the heavy silence in the air. Esther's heart clenched. She wasn't sure how much more she could bear.

"Mordecai begs for you to go before King Xerxes. He wants you to ask for mercy upon the Jews."

Esther sucked in a sharp breath. "Hegai, you know that's impossible."

His gaze softened. Yes, it was impossible. It was a death sentence to approach the king unannounced. In the House of Women, the virtue of silence had triumphed over all other protocols. She had learned that the hard way. Hegai nodded. He knew precisely what she was thinking. "I'll alert Mordecai. He must understand the gravity of his request."

Esther gnawed at her lip. Surely Mordecai would not wish to put her life at stake. They were each other's only family. Hegai returned with a piece of parchment, the ink slightly visible through the thin material.

"Your Majesty, a message from Mordecai." Hegai handed the scroll to her. She recognized Mordecai's handwriting, though the size of the letters varied with his rushed scrawls.

Hadassah, do not imagine that your residence in the palace exempts you from the king's decree. You cannot escape any more than the rest of us. If you remain silent, redemption for the Jews will arise from another place at another time, but we will perish with the rest of this generation. Perhaps that crown was set on your head for such a time as this. We need you.

Esther read Mordecai's words again. Two times. Three times. She folded the parchment neatly. She looked into the eyes of the eunuchs and maidens. The realization had already struck them. They knew who she was, and they did not hate her for it. A thousand thoughts rushed through Esther's mind, but she steadied herself with one assurance: she knew exactly what to do.

"Tell Mordecai to assemble all the Jews in Susa and begin fasting." Her voice echoed throughout the chamber with a new strength. "Starting tonight, they shall not eat or drink for three days and three nights. My maidens and I shall do the same. Only then, on the third day, will I go to the king." Esther rose to her feet. She clasped her fingers, stilling her trembling hands. "This is the command of your queen. If I perish, I perish."

Her eunuchs and maidens hastened out of the room to issue her declaration. Esther turned to the grand window behind her, sunlight streaming through the glass in brilliant orange strokes. The glow settled into her skin.

If I perish, I perish.

———

Once in the marketplace, Leila had asked how Esther would spend her last moments. The question had been posed in laughter. I would eat ten thousand cakes, she had said. I would dance through the streets without a single care, she had said. But now Esther's last moments had arrived, and there were no cakes. No streets to dance through. There were joyless banquets and empty golden cups and silent corridors.

Though her world was ending, the rest of the world didn't stop turning. The sun rose as it always did, marking the second day of fasting. Emptiness tugged at her stomach, but the burning of her heart was enough to sustain her. She hoped her maidens could say the same. They had surrendered their meals without complaint.

The whirlwind of Esther's thoughts did much to drown out her growing hunger. Her mind's eye kept returning to Haman, the source of her Abba's humiliation and the author of her people's doom. She saw the scar on his right cheek, dark and baleful like a brand of evil. His heart was set on murder. And even worse, King Xerxes trusted no one more than him.

Esther rubbed her eyes. She had not slept at all, her mind too awake and stomach too empty for rest. She tossed and turned in her plush sheets, her sweat staining the pillows with dark splotches.

The palace had fallen asleep with the rest of Susa. The silence was strange next to the clamor in her head and the cries of her people. Mordecai had assured her that the time to act was upon her. But why now? Why now, when her people were knocking at death's door? She was one girl in an empire of much stronger, much braver, much wiser men.

She tossed her blankets off, abandoning the fight for sleep. Esther sat before her vanity, studying her reflection in the dim light. Her eyes were rimmed red, the shadows beneath them like sickles reaping death. She did not look ready for valiant work, to risk her life for the sake of her people. She was tangled in a dangerous game with death. How easy it would be to simply surrender, to let the tide carry her where it would.

No. She couldn't doom her people with silence. If Mordecai was right, and she truly had been raised for such a time as this, then she couldn't turn from it now. But maybe a great calling did not come without fear.

Maybe fear was proof that it mattered.

22

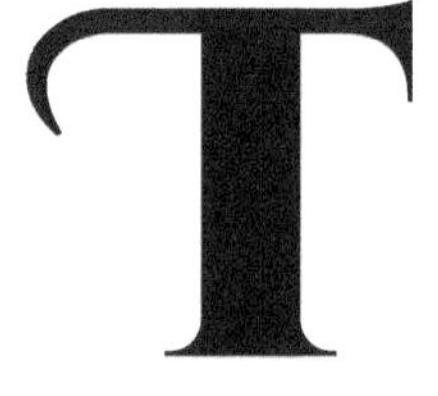HE SUN WAS MOCKING HER. Leila rose from her bed, shielding the harsh rays from her eyes. How could the light shine so brightly when she had heard the darkest news, news of the decree sentencing all Jews to death? She coughed into her elbow, cringing at the thick sound. Leila clawed for the herbal medicine at her bedside. What had the medic said? *Two swallows in the morning, two at night.* She scrunched her nose as the bitter fluid coated her throat with the taste of dirt. Leila stretched out her limbs, elated that she could finally stand on her feet without a ferocious headache.

"Leila!" Zelah walked into the room with a bowl of steaming water. She set it aside, rushing to her sister. "You shouldn't be standing up."

Leila swatted her sister's hand aside. "I'm *fine.*"

Zelah placed the back of her hand against her cheek. "No, you're not. You need to be in bed."

"I'm going to the marketplace today, *Achoti*." Leila crossed her arms defiantly. "My friends need my help."

"Sick people are not fit to be walking outside." Zelah's voice was rising now, her eyebrows knitting tighter at the center. "Are you seeing your Jewish friends?"

"Why does that matter?"

"I thought I told you to stop seeing them."

"You don't know them."

"Jews are not worth your time, Leila." Zelah felt her chest stirring with emotion. "How many times must I tell you? Royal command has sealed their death. You cannot help them."

"Why do you hate them so much?" Leila demanded. Zelah opened her mouth to say more, but she held up her hand. "Forget it. I'm leaving." Leila slammed the door shut behind her. She didn't look back.

Leila breathed in deeply, filling her lungs with the open air. The anger in her chest was slowly unravelling. With each exhale, the storm in her quieted one dark cloud at a time. Her steps grew lighter, buoyant with the simple miracle of movement after months confined to her bed. She had grown accustomed to the stale air of her room, but the clean breeze now kissing her face swept the last remnants of sickness from her bones.

It wasn't long before she spotted Shadi and Amir. The lightness of her spirits dimmed as she took in the dark expressions shadowing their faces.

"Amir! Shadi!"

The two brightened at the sound of her voice. Shadi embraced her tightly. "We're so happy you're feeling better."

Leila smiled, but her cheekbones ached from the effort. It was as if her body rejected any expression of joy. She couldn't feel happy, not at a time like this.

"You guys are in danger," Leila said. A silence stretched between them at the sobering reality. What else could she say?

"My Imma was crying last night," Amir spoke quietly.

"So was mine," Shadi said.

"It's not fair." Leila's voice took on a more fiery edge as she remembered Zelah's abhorrence of the Jews. People like her were responsible for the pain they were feeling now.

"I'm terrified," Amir said. Shadi nodded next to him. It was only then that Leila noticed their red eyes and sallow complexions.

"Do you think Queen Esther can help?" Leila asked.

"She was always so kind to us before she became queen." Amir picked at the skin of his nails, a bad habit of his that Leila had always condemned. She wondered if she would ever see it again. "Queen Esther ordered us to fast for three days. She said to hold on to hope for deliverance."

Frowning, Leila cocked her head to the side. "What's a fast?"

"It's when you don't eat food, Leila." Amir rolled his eyes, but a hint of a smile tugged at his lips.

"I haven't eaten all day," said Shadi, holding her stomach. "I'm so hungry, but it's easy to forget about it when our lives are in danger."

"Queen Esther ordered the fast?" Leila asked.

At their nods of confirmation, Leila frowned. "I wonder why she's going against the orders of the king." She shook the thought from her head. Leila took her friends' hands in hers. "I'll join you guys. I won't eat either."

Amir's eyes widened. "But you're not Jewish. You're safe either way—there's no point in starving yourself."

"I'm doing it for you guys. And for Queen Esther."

The sun had already begun its descent by the time Leila returned home. Zelah stood over a lump of dough, kneading it furiously on a wooden slab. Her head snapped to the door as Leila walked through. She brushed the flour from her hands on her robes, kicking up clouds of white powder.

"Leila, I'm sorry for lashing out earlier." Zelah knelt and reached for her sister's hands, placing a kiss on her youthful skin. "I'm making bread. You should come eat soon."

Leila backed away. "Thank you, but I can't eat anything. I'm fasting."

"Fasting for what? You're just recovering from your illness, and you need to eat well."

"Fasting for the Jews," Leila replied. Before Zelah could retaliate, Leila kissed her sister's cheek. "I'm going to bed now. Good night, *Achoti*."

Zelah watched as Leila disappeared into her room. That night, Zelah stared blankly at the walls under her sheets. The faint sound of Leila's coughing filled her ears, and the storm of her thoughts thundered in her mind. Sleep never arrived.

23

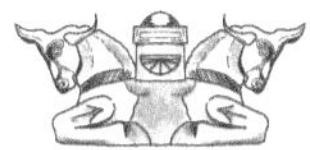

HERE WERE MANY DAYS WHEN ESTHER SAT ON HER THRONE, elevated above trembling bodies and desperate pleas for help. She never fully understood their fear. After all, she was a mere mortal. Her duty was to help, not harm. But now she was the trembling one. She did not feel like the queen of Persia—she felt like who she really was, a frightened young girl with a heart too stubborn to turn back.

The sun had risen and set on the third day. Her stomach no longer protested its hunger. Whether this was her body's quiet surrender or her fear taking over, she could not tell. Three days had taken their course, stretching like years but passing in seconds. She thought of the thousands of Jews who had fasted beside her across the empire, of their cries rising heavenward in unison. Esther drew in a slow breath, but nothing could steady her racing heart.

Her time had come. She was going to die.

Torches cast a warm glow over the throne room. Dressed in his complete royal garb, King Xerxes was a statue on his throne. The head of the golden scepter glinted menacingly white against the light. They were alone. Gone was the safety she had once felt in his presence. Xerxes was not just a man. He was the King of Kings, glowing with divine favor. Esther was playing games with deities, dancing at the gates of death.

The air was suffocating. The braziers blazed in anger, flames poised to devour her. Esther was painfully aware of every sensation. She felt her robes brushing against her shaking legs and the leaden weight of each step. Sweat gathered at her temple, and her palms grew damp. The heat of the king's gaze intensified as she drew nearer to the throne.

Her skin burned. The necklace at her throat felt like a chain pulled too tight, and she resisted the urge to tear it away. Her heart climbed into her throat as her pulse pounded louder and louder. Bile rose in her gut. The golden scepter glinted tauntingly. Esther collapsed to the ground, eyes squeezed shut. She bowed low at his feet, the floor cold against her knees.

She inhaled.

Exhaled.

Braced herself for the boom of King Xerxes's voice, for the command of her death.

Faces flashed through her mind.

She thought of Mordecai.

Leila.

Her dead mother and father.

Her people.

The earth fell into a hush. *Thud.*

Esther didn't dare to look up.

"Rise, my beloved."

Her head snapped up. From Esther's vantage point, King Xerxes appeared so above the world, so above *her*. He extended the golden scepter to her, gentleness in his gaze. Swallowing, she tremored with relief, barely restraining herself from falling back to the ground. She touched the scepter's orb with the tip of her fingers. The metal was warm against her frigid skin. Her hands were shaking. *She was alive.*

Xerxes took her hand in his, the sudden warmth electrifying. "What is your petition, Queen Esther? Request anything of me. If you desire even half my kingdom, it shall be yours."

Esther opened her mouth. *Please, my king. Spare my people, the people of Israel.* The words hung at the edge of her lips. The king was unguarded. The path was clear—she only had to step onto it.

But as the plea climbed her throat, fear wrapped a tight grip around her throat. Haman sat at the king's right hand, and the court was growing more unpredictable with each passing day. The danger of speaking abruptly was a constant shadow over her conscience. If she spoke now, Xerxes could feel accused. If Haman caught word of her request, he would twist her words. He would accelerate the genocide.

The words erupted before she could stop herself. "Should it be pleasing to you, my king, I ask that you come to a banquet that I have prepared for you and Haman tonight."

The words landed between them. Esther froze. What had she done? She couldn't afford a delay, even in the face of her fear. Every hour was a blade poised above her people's necks.

Xerxes furrowed his brow. "Of course," he said slowly, studying her face. "But surely that is not your true request. What is your petition?"

The chamber narrowed in her vision. Her throat constricted exactly as she had feared it would. If she spoke now and faltered, the moment would be lost. Esther veiled the storm inside her, shaping her lips into a gentle smile. She reached for his hand and gave it a measured squeeze. "All in due time, my king. For now, I ask only that you attend the banquet."

He nodded. "I shall call for Haman at once."

Esther breathed deeply as Xerxes roused his eunuchs. Her heart was calming at last. Haman swiftly entered the chamber, the royal signet ring glinting on his finger. He bowed and smiled brilliantly at Esther. His scar creased with the rise of his cheekbones.

"It is an honor, Your Majesty."

Esther's lips curved as the man who thirsted for her people's blood lifted her hand to his lips. If only he knew he kissed the blood of her Abba, the very man he hated most.

"The honor is mine, Haman."

24

**OU HAVE THE MOST EXQUISITE TASTES, YOUR HIGHNESSES."** The banquet was nothing short of Persian royalty. Platters of chicken and fish glistened on copper plates, and mountainous rolls of bread towered in bowls. Every cheese and fruit sat in the glittering display. Carefully avoiding the meat, Esther plucked a grape from its stem.

"How you flatter us, Haman." King Xerxes bellowed in laughter. Esther noted how quickly his wine goblet had depleted. "But, of course, we wouldn't settle for less."

"None can rival your glory, King Xerxes," Haman continued. "Even the Greeks, for all of their supposed cunning, were humbled by your armies. How fortunate Persia is to have such a king."

"You speak well," Xerxes clapped his hands, summoning more wine. "Few appreciate the courage it took to march on their wretched cities."

"And we mustn't forget how the gods have blessed us with a glorious queen."

Esther smiled faintly. She could not bring herself to pretend that this man hadn't set out to destroy her brothers and sisters. "You are most generous, Haman. But perhaps the truest glory is in protecting those who cannot protect themselves." She gazed pointedly at Haman, her smile sickly sweet.

"Beautiful *and* wise," Haman raised his goblet before turning to Xerxes. His scar had never appeared darker. "You are a lucky man, King Xerxes."

"Indeed." The king's gaze lingered on Esther, his eyes slightly hooded from the wine. "You have yet to tell me your true request, Queen Esther. What is your petition? Even if you desire half of my kingdom, it shall be given to you."

Esther opened her mouth to seal the fate of the Jews, to reveal Haman's great evil and the pain he had inflicted. She caught Haman's gaze, his obsidian eyes glinting at her with startling directness. Her throat closed. Doubt slicked her palms, and her pulse thrashed in her neck. Something wasn't right. It wasn't the proper time. But hadn't she used the same excuse last time? How long would she submit to fear?

Esther coughed into her fist. She apologized before taking a sip of wine. She lifted the goblet to conceal a part of her face, commanding her heart to slow, her hands to stop trembling.

"If I have found favor with Your Majesty," Esther began, looking at King Xerxes, "I invite you and Haman to another banquet I shall prepare tomorrow. Then I will do as you please, my king, and reveal my true petition." She breathed a sigh of relief, stealing a glance at Haman to see if he had noticed her panic. His expression remained unchanged. Another sigh.

King Xerxes took her hand in his, thrusting his wine goblet into the air. "Very well. To Queen Esther and the people of Persia."

Haman raised his goblet. "To Your Majesties and the people of Persia."

Esther raised her goblet. "To the people of Persia."

———

The room was drenched in dusk. The velvet curtains framing the lattice windows of Haman's bedchambers rustled like secret whispers in the night. Zeresh's jasmine scent weighed heavily in the air. Haman drank in the sight of his wife sprawled out on the silk sheets. Her gown slipped carelessly off one shoulder, and her midnight hair cascaded loosely down the curve of her neck.

Haman stood by the fireplace, watching as the flaming tongues flickered through the air. A harsh glow illuminated the marble floors. His palms were in fists at his sides, knuckles white and heart burning even fiercer than the fire before him.

He replayed the scene again and again. He left the palace after Queen Esther's banquet, heavy with wine and satisfaction. The queen had chosen him alone to dine beside herself and King Xerxes, and she had invited him again. The thought swelled in his chest. As he passed through the king's gate, he noticed an older man standing near the golden entrance. Haman slowed, anticipating the familiar bend of a spine and lowered eyes. Men always bowed. The king and queen favored him, and as chief among his advisors, he was practically royalty. When the man did not move, Haman snapped in fury. He turned and saw Mordecai, the same wretched Jew who had refused him months ago. The sight fueled his anger from a flickering match to an explosive fire. Mordecai's face was calm, almost indifferent. His quiet defiance awakened something wild in Haman's chest.

Though he had called upon his family and closest companions for another round of wine in his home, it did nothing to quell his anger. It was not right for someone of his stature to be scorned by the scum of the earth. Mordecai's face grew more vivid in his mind's eye as Haman stared into the fire. He imagined the Jew's face in the flames.

"What troubles you, my love?" Zeresh called from the bed. Her voice dripped like honey. "You've been tense since you returned home."

Haman clenched the hem of his robes in his fist. "Mordecai. It's that Jewish man who refuses to bow before me." His voice was getting louder, but he hardly cared. "He believes he is above the universe. All the Jews see themselves atop a hill, but their true worth lies below the earth. Their forefathers inflicted great pain on mine, and they think themselves above us."

He heard Zeresh rise from the bed, her bare feet soundless against the marble. She pressed herself against him and brought her hands to his chest, her fingers cool against Haman's rising heat. "You forget Mordecai is not the one who wears King Xerxes's ring, my lord."

Haman glanced at the golden band. "I can never be satisfied so long as Mordecai sits at the king's gate."

Zeresh turned her husband around to face her. She brought her hands up to his neck, pressing her lips against his ear. "Then kill him."

Haman froze. "What?"

"You agonize over a problem that can be easily fixed," Zeresh continued, slithering back into the bedsheets. "The Jews will perish, regardless. But if you wish to see Mordecai's end now, ask King Xerxes to have a gallows made in the morning for him. Then, you can dine with the king and queen as a liberated soul."

"What if the king refuses my request?"

Zeresh laughed. "Xerxes is easily swayed. That's why he needs you, and he will hardly turn down a request from you. You are his closest confidant."

Haman turned to her fully now. He slid under the covers alongside her, pressing a kiss to her collarbone.

"Your anxieties are groundless. You'll be feared and celebrated in the streets," Zeresh purred. "And the Jews shall finally answer to a greater god."

Heart pounding, Haman kissed her honeyed lips. As he slid Zeresh's nightgown down her shoulder, something uncoiled inside him. Something monstrous that licked its lips for blood and justice.

25

THE SCRATCHING OF INK *AGAINST PARCHMENT FILLED THE AIR. Xerxes sat quietly as his scribe hastily recorded his words. The night was still. His excursion in the* garden with Queen Esther had enlivened his spirits. As King of Kings, he deserved nothing less than perfection, and the gods had gifted him with a perfect queen. Her walk, the part of her lips, the regal calm of her words. Esther was enchanting. Even as she revealed the threat to his life, she spoke in gentle melodies.

"My lord, what was the name of the man who discovered this dreadful attempt on your life?" The scribe looked up from the parchment, interrupting the king's thoughts.

"Mordecai," Xerxes said, remembering Esther's account. "His name is Mordecai."

The value of an object tended to increase with scarcity. For the king of Persia, nothing was scarcer than rest. Months of plotting against his enemies had kept him late into the night, poring over maps and debating with his commanders. Sometimes, he had even seen the sunrise before collapsing in his chambers.

There was no reason for sleep to be elusive. His people had emerged victorious. He had overpowered the Greeks. Though Xerxes suspected the war was not over, it would be months before their forces fully recovered. This was the time to shut his eyes and surrender to rest. Yet he tossed and turned in a cold sweat, tousling the sheets fitfully.

The moon hung high, its soft glow touching Xerxes's eyelids through the window. *Sleep*, it seemed to say. But the king simply could not. He released a long breath, beckoning to the nearest guard.

"Call someone here to read one of the palace records from the scribes' keep. If this cannot put me to sleep, I am truly a hopeless case."

"Right away, Your Majesty."

Xerxes was a hopeless case. Nothing was duller than the technicalities of palace functions and procedures. Who requested audiences in the palace, what province they were from, their family background, whether their petition had been fulfilled, the details of their grievances…

"It has been discovered that the palace guards Bigthan and Teresh planned an assassination against His Majesty, having obtained unofficial documents from an undetermined source. A message from Her Highness Queen Esther on behalf of Mordecai of Susa—"

Xerxes paused, tilting his head. "Repeat that."

A memory flashed through his mind, a memory of Xerxes beside his scribe as he retold Esther's discovery. He had strolled through the courtyard with her before she revealed the danger. A magical night, Xerxes remembered fondly. Two guards had planned to murder him. But there was something else, something that bothered him.

"What was the name of the man who saved my life?" Xerxes asked.

"Mordecai the Jew."

Mordecai. The name sounded strangely familiar. "Has anything been done to reward this man?"

"Nothing has been done," the eunuch said. "Would you like me to continue, Your Highness?"

Xerxes waved his hand dismissively. "Is there anyone trustworthy in the court at this hour that I can consult?"

"I shall summon someone, my lord."

Xerxes sighed to himself. He prided himself on never owing debts to anyone. Mordecai saved his life, the ultimate debt. How had this slipped past him?

The door creaked open as the eunuch returned alongside Haman. Xerxes smiled at the sight of his Supreme Chief. The perfect voice to call upon.

"Great King." Haman bowed deeply.

"I have a dilemma, Haman," Xerxes began. "I have neglected to reward someone in my court who deserves the highest honor. What do you recommend be done for this man?"

The edges of Haman's mouth curled upward. "If this man has gained your favor, then the greatest glory should be given to him. He should be presented with the royal robes and horse of the king, and the crown should be placed on his head. The most noble princes should escort him through the streets of Susa, and all will declare his name in the streets. This is the only way to truly honor the man."

King Xerxes nodded, clapping his hands together. "Your proposal is excellent, Haman. I knew you would not disappoint."

"Of course, Your Majesty."

"We must get to work. Take my robes and saddle the horse. Do all that you have said for Mordecai the Jew. Once the sun rises, you shall find him before the palace gates. I trust you to make this ceremony worthy of the gods."

Haman smiled, though something barely discernible shifted in his expression. "As you wish, my lord."

———

Cheering. Esther groggily opened her eyes, shielding the incoming sun from her eyes. Hollering and whistling and clapping flooded her ears. She crawled out of her covers in a daze. What could have aroused the city at such an early hour?

She walked out to the terrace in her bedchambers overlooking Susa. The sight before her snapped her out of her daze instantly. There he was. Her Abba, waving on a valiant white horse. He rode in luxurious crimson robes, the fabric billowing around him like royalty. The crown upon his head glinted in the morning light. He was led by a troop of lavishly dressed nobles and…*Haman?* Esther rubbed her eyes. Surely this was a dream. But there was no mistaking the king's ring on Haman's finger. The voice booming in the streets belonged undeniably to the Supreme Chief of Persia.

"All honor to Mordecai the Jew! All honor to the man exalted by our Great King!"

The city square overflowed with people, their hands clapping and voices joining in a chorus of cheers. Esther's jaw dropped to the floor. Laughter spilled out of her before she could contain it. Esther clutched her stomach, unable to control the joy streaming through her lips.

Nothing could have been more absurd. Haman was hailing her Abba in the streets, the most devout Jew she knew. Esther had never smiled so brilliantly. Her cheekbones ached, but this was a pain she welcomed.

"Your Majesty, may I join you?"

Esther turned. Her eyes widened at the sight of King Xerxes in his royal robes. She looked down at her sleeping attire, suddenly self-conscious of her tangled hair and dark circles.

"My king, what are you doing here?" she asked. "This is hardly appropriate."

He stepped toward the balcony, leaning over the banister as they looked upon the cheering masses. "I apologize, Esther. I simply wanted to celebrate with you before we are both swallowed by our daily obligations." He sighed deeply, intertwining their fingers. "I never thanked you for informing me of the plot against my life. And I never honored the man who revealed such wickedness to you. I am indebted to you both."

"Does this mean you shall also parade me along the streets?" Esther remarked playfully.

King Xerxes laughed, and Esther realized it was the first time she had heard him laugh so freely. The sound was deep. Even comforting. "You don't strike me as the type who would particularly enjoy that," he said with a smile. "But just say the word, and I'll have ten thousand horses parading you around."

Esther shivered. "Let's keep them in the stables."

She wished she could pause this moment forever. She was a queen beside her king, looking out upon their people as they cheered for her Abba. Just for a moment, she could pretend that a decree of death did not loom over her people. Pretend that she wouldn't have to inform Xerxes of Haman's wickedness. Pretend that her life wouldn't end if she failed to speak tonight at the banquet.

She could pretend.

———

Construction was almost complete. The wooden stakes loomed behind Haman's house, the cracks and patterns of the wood visible through the window of his dining space. A bundle of rope rested in front of the planks, soon to be tied into a noose. He had never received the king's permission for the gallows, but he didn't see why he needed it. He was the Supreme Chief.

Zeresh sat beside her husband, tracing patterns on his thigh. But there was no consoling his wounded ego. Even his sons, who normally uplifted their father by boasting of their achievements, couldn't soothe his bruised heart.

It simply wasn't possible. Haman must have transgressed the gods somehow. Nothing else could explain this tragedy. The previous night, he had ventured to the king's court to request gallows for Mordecai, but the man he intended to hang was the man King Xerxes ordered him to honor. No man had done more for the king than Haman. Mordecai was a criminal, a rebellious disease unworthy of glory. Haman's voice was hoarse from shouting the Jew's name in the streets. His feet were sore from walking, and his cheekbones ached from forced smiles. But most painful of all, his chest seared with utter humiliation.

"May the gods forgive me for whatever wrong I have committed against them," Haman said. "I cannot make sense of this. What has Mordecai done that could cause King Xerxes to honor him above me, his closest confidant? I have poured my soul into serving this empire. What has Mordecai done? Tell me, what has he done?"

Aridai, the eldest of his nine sons, slammed his fist against the table. "This is why it would have been better if those wretched guards had not failed to assassinate Xerxes while they had the chance. Did you not take every step to ensure their jobs could be completed seamlessly? Those forged parchments cost us much."

"The past is in the past, my son. Those useless guards do not warrant the blame here. It is Mordecai the Jew," Haman seethed. "It is *always* Mordecai the Jew."

"If the king continues to elevate Mordecai in such a way," Zeresh spoke. "Then it will not be long before you are the one bowing at his feet, husband. You must do whatever it takes to prevent this."

Haman opened his mouth to say more, but suddenly the door burst open. Two of the king's eunuchs marched into the space, armed with sharpened spears.

Haman shot from his seat. "What is the meaning of this?"

"My lord, we are to escort you to Queen Esther's banquet. The king and queen are waiting for you."

Haman silently cursed. Amid the day's spectacle, he had completely forgotten about the banquet. And King Xerxes detested tardiness. He hastened beside the eunuchs out of the house. Haman stole a glance over his shoulder before stepping through the door, catching a final glimpse of Zeresh's face, his sons hovered around the table, and the shadow of the gallows through the window.

26

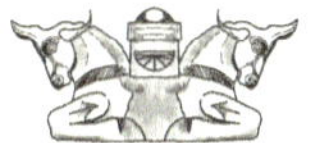

 TREE WAS KNOWN BY ITS **FRUIT,** and exuberance was the fruit of wealth. In the palace, no fruit ever grew so abundantly. Esther felt small within the splendor, like an insect staring up at the vast world. The banquet she had arranged with Hegai and her maidens was a spectacle of indulgence. Rubies and emeralds glittered along the carved reliefs that bordered the walls. Gold-threaded tapestries cascaded between soaring columns. Low tables of polished cedar gleamed beneath platters of figs split open like jewels. Pomegranates bled into silver bowls, and roasted lamb glazed with honey and spice.

Esther sat quietly beside the king. A crystal vessel stood silently before her. She faced her reflection in the wine, her face rippling in the deep red. Her darkened brows and kohl-lined eyes stared back at her, cool and detached. Esther concealed her trembling hands inside her lap. She could delay no longer. Tonight, her people would be saved, or Haman would dance on their graves in triumph.

That was, if Haman even appeared. The shadows were moving across the walls, and he was still nowhere in sight.

King Xerxes huffed impatiently. "If he does not appear within the hour—"

The doors burst open. Haman surged into the room, erupting with apologies. He lowered himself at Xerxes's feet until his forehead kissed the ground. Esther clenched her robes in her fists.

"With this magnificent display before us, it would be wrong to taint the night so soon," Xerxes said. "But you will not keep your king and queen waiting again, Haman."

Again. By the end of the night, hopefully there wouldn't be an opportunity of *again* for Haman.

"I shall die before I disobey you, Great King."

Esther looked upon the lavish spread. The fruits glistened lustrously beneath the torchlight, but the knot in her stomach strangled any trace of hunger. She forced a sip of wine, its sweetness turning sharp against the nausea rising in her throat. Across the table, the king and Haman laughed easily, their voices warm and untroubled. Their goblets met in bright, ringing clinks. Her stomach lurched.

"You have done great things for your people, King Xerxes," Haman grinned. He took a measured sip of wine. "I can hardly imagine the burdens of royalty."

Xerxes waved a dismissive hand, though the praise pulled his features into a simper. "The burdens are many," he said. "An empire does not hold itself together."

"Just so," Haman replied smoothly. "The task becomes especially difficult when certain forces resist that unity. I'm sure some still refuse to bend to your authority." His gaze flickered briefly to Esther before returning to the king. "It is no small mercy to bring order where there is disorder."

Esther's fingers tightened around the stem of her cup.

Xerxes reclined against the cushions. "You're speaking of the decree."

"It was a necessary measure." Haman slid the edge of his knife along the lamb's meat. He chewed in slow bites. Swallowed. "A kingdom thrives when its people move as one."

Esther set her goblet down before her trembling hand betrayed her. "What do you say of those who walk a different path?"

Haman's smile did not falter. "If they are loyal, they have nothing to fear. You are a wise ruler, Queen Esther. You understand the value of harmony. It is only those who resist that endanger this peace."

The chamber felt smaller. The torches burned too brightly, the flames hot against her skin.

Xerxes placed a hand over Esther's cold one. "Are you alright, my queen? You seem troubled."

Haman continued, almost thoughtfully, "Surely Your Majesty agrees. It is better to uproot a problem entirely than allow it to fester."

Esther rose slowly from her seat.

"Indeed, Haman," she began. "It is better to uproot the problem, to kill the virus before it spreads." She turned to King Xerxes. "My king, you asked for my true request. If I have found favor in your sight, grant me my life, and spare my people."

Silence fell. She thought of Mordecai's face, of him being praised in the streets, and she suddenly realized she wanted nothing more than to see him again. She wanted to see her people rejoice without shame.

"Great King, you recently honored a Jew in the streets, a man named Mordecai who saved your life. Mordecai is my father," Esther continued, lifting her gaze. "I am an Israelite, a descendant of an ancient tribe. My people have been sold into destruction, to be slain and utterly annihilated. My father was humiliated and punished for standing up to this great wickedness. If this evildoer's malice comes to fruition, I will perish alongside the good people of this kingdom."

Rage possessed the king's features. "Who is he?" he boomed. "Who dares to do such a thing?"

Esther's eyes fell to Haman's hand. The king's signet ring glinted on his finger, the very seal that had sanctioned her death. She turned to his face, drained of its color. Her resolve steeled. He had written the fate of her people with that ring. Whatever chance of redemption he once possessed had withered the moment he used the king's authority to condemn the innocent.

Esther lifted her chin.

"It is your closest confidant," she said, her voice gaining strength with every word. "The man who celebrates as your people cry in anguish."

She pointed.

"The man of wickedness is this evil Haman."

———

A flurry of activity ensued. King Xerxes slammed his hands on the table, fires blazing in his eyes. He stormed out of the chamber, his robes sweeping behind him in a raging wave. Eyes wide with terror, Haman dove for Esther. He groveled at her feet, clutching her robes.

"Your Majesty, I beg you!" Haman cried. His white knuckles tremored. She kicked her leg in protest, but his grip only tightened. "Had I known you were one of them, I would have never issued the decree. The proclamation can be revoked, I swear it!"

"You have committed an unforgivable act, Haman." Esther's tone was sharper than a blade. "Your evil cannot be redeemed."

"I beg you, Your Highness." Haman pushed Esther back into the velvet cushions. Her heart sparked with fear. He clawed closer until she could see the beads of sweat forming at his temples. "I have a family. What will my wife and sons do without me?" She threw her force against him, but he remained unmoving. "You must convince the king to have mercy upon me. I never intended to harm you, Queen Esther."

It was as if his fingers were forged of iron. Esther had never felt such disdain. "My people and I are one. When you wish harm on them, you wish harm on me."

But Haman would not relent. He clutched her body in crazed desperation, fingers digging into the fabric at her waist. His pleas tumbled over one another in wild abandon, and the scent of wine clung to his breath. Where were the eunuchs?

Panic seized her. Her heart did not calm even as two pairs of hands wrenched Haman backward with brutal force. He cried out in violent thrashing, but even in his frenzy, he could not break their hold. His feet scraped against the marble as he was dragged away.

The doors flew open. Xerxes strode in, fury blazing across his face. "As if you could not worsen your transgressions, you even assault the queen in my presence?" Xerxes roared.

Esther sat on the floor with a hand over her chest. She peered at the hem of her robes, ruined by Haman's futile attempts at redemption. Nausea swirled through her at the dark splotches of his tears against the silk. King Xerxes folded his hands over hers, his gentleness like still waters. "Are you alright, Esther?"

She nodded, exhaling slowly. Esther could hardly bring herself to look at him. The gravity of her declaration struck her. She had unveiled the one secret meant to remain in darkness forever.

"Your Majesty." Esther forced herself to look into his eyes. "I have deceived you by concealing the entire truth. I swore to my father that I would never discuss my heritage, and I have broken that promise, too. You must see me differently."

"You are my queen," he replied. "That is more than enough. And had I known Mordecai was your caretaker, I would have bestowed him with the highest honor even before he saved my life." He brushed a tear from her cheek with the pad of his thumb. "Everything will be alright, Esther."

A guard who had carried Haman out surged back into the chamber. Xerxes rose from the couch, his features settling into stone once more.

"What is your business, Harbonah?" King Xerxes said. "What has been done with Haman?"

"Great King, my guards have investigated Haman's dwelling, and we discovered an immense gallows outside the space. It was constructed illegally for Mordecai, the same man who saved your life."

Esther's heart hardened.

"Hang Haman on the gallows," Xerxes declared. His tone was calm, but the simmering rage beneath it sent a chill down Esther's spine. "Let him swing, and let his blood water the grass beneath his feet."

"As you wish, Great King."

27

HE WOOD CREAKED BENEATH
HIS BARE FEET. The sky above
stretched out in a clear, vast sea. His
shoulders burned under the sun's
battering rays.

The rope was rough against Haman's neck. The skin of his Adam's apple grew red and raw, and his loose hair matted the side of his face. A phantom weight settled where the king's ring had once shone on his finger.

Zeresh's eyes were bloodshot. She cowered on the floor and clutched her sons' hands, wailing with the sound of a thousand sirens. The eunuchs stood stone-faced at their side.

His vision was blurry. Scarlet veins cracked through the whites of his eyes. Surrounded by a shield of palace guards, King Xerxes and Queen Esther watched at a distance. Her gaze never strayed from his face.

Haman closed his eyes. Faint cheers rode in the breeze from the city square. *Mordecai,* they were chanting. *All hail Mordecai the Jew!* His Imma's face flashed through his mind. He saw the curve of her brows, the hollow of her cheekbones, the ghostly pallor of her dead form.

He opened his eyes, breathing deeply. The air tasted faintly metallic. His scar stung. He frowned. His scar hadn't ached in years.

The rope tightened, and his feet left the floor. The bones of his neck shattered with a loud *snap.*

The last thing Haman saw was Queen Esther's unwavering eyes, cold and immovable as stone.

28

HE STYLUS STRUCK THE **TABLE.** Esther cradled her head in her hands, eyes blurring over the parchment before her. The letter to the princesses of India was long overdue. After the abrupt end to their meeting, she had meant to reach out to secure a reunion. But between Haman's downfall and the weight of her obligations, sleep had become a distant memory.

"You look wonderful for a sleep-deprived queen."

"How you flatter me, Hegai." Esther deadpanned. "What is your business?"

"I come with two missions," Hegai continued. "The first is to assess your sanity. After hearing all that transpired last night, I came here immediately."

Esther had stood before death. Mordecai had barely escaped danger. She had exposed Haman, and she had witnessed his last breath. She hadn't slept properly in weeks. And yet, the king stood with her. Her Abba was alive.

"I've never been better."

Hegai laughed. "Graceful as always. My second matter is to summon you before King Xerxes. You're needed in the throne room, my lady." He held out his arm. "Come with me."

Esther placed her palm on his forearm as they traversed the corridor. "Hegai, do you think of me any differently?"

There was no need for clarification. "Yes, I think of you differently," he began. "I did not believe my respect for you could increase, but you've corrected me." A smile touched his lips. "Heritage alone does not make a noble queen, nor does it make a noble heart. You possess both."

Esther's shoulders eased. She laughed quietly. "I am indebted to you, Hegai. And you should smile more often. It suits you."

He raised an eyebrow. "Is that a royal command?"

"I can make it one."

"Please spare me from that burden."

———

Nothing compared to the relief of a secret unearthed. Esther's muscles no longer tensed at her neck, and her stomach had untwisted its bundle of nerves. As she entered the throne room and beheld the affection in Xerxes's gaze, she couldn't contain her smile.

"Queen Esther," said Xerxes, rising from his throne. He pressed a kiss to her forehead. "An esteemed guest is on his way, and I would like you to greet him. But before he arrives, there's something you must know—after Haman's sentence, his family went into hiding. We haven't seen them since his execution. In their absence, however, his estate remains empty. I have no need for it, so you may do with it as you please."

Esther bowed her head. "Thank you, my king."

In truth, the palace already afforded her more than she required. Another estate meant little to her. But as the words left Xerxes's lips, a thought solidified in her heart. Haman's house would not remain a monument to cruelty. She knew the perfect host to take over, to transform the evil that had transpired within.

Xerxes settled back into his seat and motioned to the eunuchs. The great doors swung open. Mordecai stepped through the threshold, flanked by three of the king's personal guards. Morning light flooded the throne room behind him, illuminating his silhouette as the rays caught on the edges of his body. Relief crashed over Esther, fierce and overwhelming. She bit her tongue, fighting the urge to leap from her throne and bury her face in his chest.

"King Xerxes." Her Abba bowed. "Queen Esther."

"Rise, Mordecai of Susa."

He stood.

King Xerxes's features morphed into a smile, a rare sight in the throne room. Esther noticed the signet ring had returned to his hand. The golden band winked. "I can hardly treat the caretaker of my queen as a mere subject of the empire," said Xerxes. "Queen Esther tells me you are like a father to her."

"Yes, Your Majesty." Mordecai's gaze caught Esther's, and her chest swelled. "She is my only family."

"You have raised the most important woman in my court," continued Xerxes. "You saved my life, and you saw evil in a place all of us were blind to, including me." Xerxes slid the ring off his finger. "I cannot think of a more honorable man to bestow this power upon."

"Thank you, Great King."

Esther watched in quiet awe as two distant worlds collided. Her Abba, a man of modest means and stained garments. Her husband, robed in splendor and anointed with wine. Humility and empire, side by side.

Esther cleared her throat. "If I may, my king, I would like to say one last word."

At Xerxes's nod, she continued. "There is a great house south of the palace at the edge of the city square. It once belonged to Haman, the fallen enemy of our people. As it was placed in my charge, I now place it in yours, Abba."

Mordecai fell to his knees, gratitude bringing his frame low against the marble. Esther's chest tightened. She longed to run to him, to be gathered into his embrace as she had the last time he entered the throne room. But that time, King Xerxes had not been present. Esther remained seated, spine straight and hands folded. Her heart pressed painfully against her ribs. She would see him again. The thought comforted her.

Until it didn't.

Her breath faltered. Her pulse surged violently in her ears. The room seemed to tilt, the air thinning as though siphoned away. Her lungs strained against the sudden weight in her chest.

She wouldn't see him again. In the rush of Haman's exposure and execution, she had allowed herself to believe the danger had ended, that death had buried his decree with him. But no. Persian law held that a decree sealed with the king's ring could not be revoked, not even by the king himself. She flung a hand to her chest in a desperate move to calm her heart. The month was waning. Adar crept closer with each passing day. And when it arrived, the Jews across the empire would still stand condemned, left to the mercy of the Persians.

King Xerxes leapt to her behind Mordecai, placing a hand on her shoulder. Mordecai cupped her face in his hands.

"My queen," said King Xerxes. "Are you alright? Are you ill?"

Esther fell to the ground at his feet, tears flowing in streams down her cheeks. "My king, it struck me that my people are still doomed. Haman's law is irrevocable, and the Jews will be destroyed. I beg you to avert his evil scheme. I hadn't realized the decree was still in place. How could I have been so foolish—"

Xerxes took her hands, bringing Esther to her feet. He brushed the tears from her cheeks.

"Queen Esther, I would battle the gods for you," began Xerxes. "But even I am not above Persian law. No law that has been sealed with the king's ring can be revoked."

"There must be some way to save them." Esther's throat was raw with tears, but her voice resounded strongly. "Let a new decree counter Haman's evil scheme. I refuse to let calamity fall upon the Israelites. I could not bear to watch my brothers and sisters be slaughtered."

Xerxes nodded, shifting his gaze to Mordecai. "You now bear my ring. Write to the Jews as you see fit with Queen Esther, and seal it in my name. Do not worry, my queen." He took Esther's hands in his. "We will prevail."

They wasted no time. When Esther imagined reuniting with Mordecai, she had not envisioned the scene she now found herself in: seated in a palace chamber surrounded by eunuchs, drafting a letter to all the Jews of the empire. Esther had forgotten her Abba's eloquence, how brilliantly he commanded a room. Her eyes kept drifting to the golden ring. It was unnerving to see the band on Mordecai's finger; she had grown so used to seeing it on Haman's bejeweled hands.

Esther scrutinized Mordecai's decree. Read it again. And again. She did not remember how many times she examined the words. All she knew was that the fire of darkness Haman had spread throughout her kingdom was to be extinguished with another fire, the fire of light.

Mordecai pressed the king's ring firmly into the warm wax upon the parchment. The insignia left an indelible mark. Esther watched as Xerxes's couriers gathered the sealed decrees and hurried through the great doors, sent out to every corner of the empire. Jews and Persians alike felt the shift in the air. For on the thirteenth day of Adar, blood was to flood the streets. Not Jewish blood, but the blood of all who rose against the people of Mordecai. The blood of those with hate in their hearts. The Persians were not safe. The Israelites would fight. Fire to fire, blood to blood.

A great cry reverberated throughout King Xerxes's empire, for the Israelites had been saved! How could this be? The oppressed were to become the liberated. Esther retreated to the balcony of her bedchamber, looking out as her people flooded the streets with hollers and tears of joy. Strangers hugged one another like the closest of brothers. And as she watched Mordecai emerge from the palace gates in brilliant blue robes and with the crown upon his brow, Esther gazed at the vast sea of the sky and smiled.

———

With a crown on your head, you are expected to walk gracefully. But the royal life will always thrust something at you that will knock you off your feet.

Hegai had imparted much wisdom in the harem, but that one lesson had never left her. From the moment the crown had touched her head, Esther's life had unraveled into a chain of unforeseen turns. Expect the unexpected, she had learned. As she slipped through the carved doorway into the back chamber of the House of Women, she allowed herself a small, knowing breath. Perhaps it was time to expect the unexpected more often.

Hegai remained the caretaker of the king's maidens, and after some investigation, Esther discovered that several of the young women she had once trained beside stayed in the harem, waiting for the next window of opportunity to see the king. Technically, Esther wasn't supposed to be here—the harem belonged only to Xerxes. But she had come with a purpose. When she had confided her plan to Hegai, he did not question her. He led her to the back entrance, manipulating the lock with a brass key.

"Make it quick, before the king arrests me," he said. "I'll be here."

The harem felt eerily unchanged. It looked the same as it had the night she was chosen. Silk sheets hung from the ceiling, and the scent of perfume hung heavy in the air, flooding her senses. Faint laughter chimed in the distance. Young girls, no more than twenty, lounged on couches in sheer silk robes. She recognized nearly all of them. It did not take long for Esther to find Kyra, sitting with her back to the wall, armed with a handful of grapes. Esther's heart twinged. It was as if time had frozen. Her sleek hair and obsidian eyes remained ever the same.

Kyra rose from the ground, her eyes widening. "Esther?" Her voice caught between awe and disbelief. But she suddenly seemed to remember who she was speaking to. Kyra lowered her head to the ground, as did the surrounding maidens. "Queen Esther." Her voice sounded strained.

"Please," Esther said, taking her hands. "Just Esther."

She could feel the gaze of the other maidens sliding over her crown, fixating on her jeweled sash and luxurious silken robes. She felt the weight of their stares, sensed envy greener than poison.

Kyra pulled away. Esther's heart ached at the distance between them, but she didn't make another motion forward. "It's been two years, Esther. What business could you have with us now?" Kyra's voice was rising. "I've been stuck in this rotting place, and you never thought to contact me. The king never comes to see us anymore. We are wasting away, jewels left behind in the dust."

Esther's heart caged in on itself. "Kyra—"

"I didn't say I was finished, *Your Majesty*." She said the title like a taunt, like something childish. Her voice was taking on a poisonous edge, a malice that frightened Esther, where she was accustomed to friendly affection. "I didn't think I was so bold as to hope for one letter. Just one update from a dear friend. But I suppose a mere whore of the king is not worth your time."

"Kyra," Esther said more firmly.

"Were you too busy swimming in your wealth? Were you sighing with pleasure in the king's arms? Gorging on palace food and getting drunk on wine while the rest of us strive for fulfillment?"

"That's enough!" Esther breathed deeply, looking in her friend's blade-like eyes. "Kyra, I've done you wrong. You're right. But I'm here for something far more important than you or I."

"Of course you are," she sneered. "You're always representing the greater good, aren't you?"

Esther pressed on. She felt the eyes of everyone in the room on her, but somehow it emboldened her to speak louder. "As the queen, I am prohibited from entering this space. Even now, I risk punishment by speaking to you. I came here to warn you."

The intensity of Kyra's countenance had not diminished. "We are not ignorant of what is taking place in the city. The situation of the Jews has improved, hasn't it? What is there to warn us about?"

"The situation of the Jews has improved, but yours have been put in jeopardy," Esther began. The mood of the space shifted. Apprehensive, the girls exchanged glances. "It is no longer the Jews who will be destroyed, but all who stand against them. On the thirteenth day of Adar, blood will fill the streets. Your friends and families are not safe from this violence."

Esther breathed deeply. "Join the cause of the Jews." There. She had said it. "Fight alongside the Jews, and your lives will be preserved."

"But are we not safe in the harem?" one maiden asked. "Surely we will not be asked to fight."

"No one will be spared. Alert your families," continued Esther. "If you choose to remain silent, it may cost your life."

"A unique sort of arrogance has possessed you if you believe I would listen to you now." Kyra laughed, each bitter intonation like a blow to Esther's chest. "Queen or peasant, what makes you think I value what you say anymore?"

"Don't value my words, but value your life," Esther said. Frustration boiled in her chest, but she forced it to calm. "You're not a fool, Kyra. You know there's unrest in the empire. And the only way we'll find peace is by siding with the Jews."

"You will find no allegiance here, Esther," Kyra refused to look at her. She was shaking in subtle tremors. "Leave. Leave to your gilded palace before I force you to."

Esther grimaced, her heart sinking. She had expected recognition, even warmth, but the maidens' gazes were distant. The air was thick with something colder than silence.

"You're a greater fool than I was, Kyra."

All heads snapped to the back of the room. Zelah stood in the corner, blending into the shadow of the wall. Esther's heart jolted in surprise. She looked markedly better than she had during their last encounter in the throne room, when she had threatened Esther with her heritage. Her eyes had brightened, and her hair had returned to its perfect sheen.

Kyra raised an eyebrow. Her voice dripped with contempt. "Do not challenge me, Zelah."

"My sister almost died from illness, but Queen Esther saved her life." Zelah stepped out of the darkness. "When she recovered, she fasted with the Jews. I will never fully understand my sister's devotion to the Israelites, but I cannot rest well standing against her." Zelah stared at Esther intently. "If it is the queen's orders that all against the Jews will die, then you will perish. Do not think you are safe, Kyra."

Esther struggled to keep her jaw from dropping. Where had this come from? She gazed intently at Zelah. Her resemblance to Leila had never appeared stronger. A taut silence stretched between them. Kyra exhaled slowly, the weight of unspoken resentment hanging in her words. "And you, Esther?" she asked, her voice edged with lingering bitterness. "Will you also stand with the Jews?"

"I penned the decree affirming the Jews' in the destruction of their enemies. So, yes, I stand with the Jews, as does the rest of the palace." Esther locked eyes with Kyra. It pained her to be regarded with such hardened gazes where laughter and joy once resided. "Fight with the Israelites. The decision is yours, but I do not wish to see you perish so soon."

The other maidens looked to Kyra, anticipating her next move. Esther suddenly realized that she had somehow become a leader over the House of Women. She shot a glance at Esther, her arms crossed.

"Do not think this means I forgive you," she began. "We will do as you say, but on one condition."

"Even if it is up to half the kingdom, it shall be given to you."

"Free us," she said. "Free us from this gilded prison, and we will do as you say."

"I will bring your petition to the king," Esther said. "Your request shall surely be granted to you. Thank you, Kyra. Zelah." Esther regarded the two girls intently. Though Kyra didn't return the look, Zelah gave her a solemn nod. It was enough. And as much as she didn't express it, Kyra never strayed from her word. Esther would have to make it up to her fully someday, but she knew a small part of Kyra, though begrudgingly, had already forgiven her.

Esther stepped out of the harem, picking up the hem of her gown on the way out.

"Are you alright, Queen Esther?" Hegai asked.

She smiled.

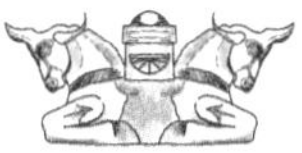

The thirteenth day of Adar

**ORNING BROKE WITH SILENCE.** The streets of Susa lay eerily hushed, every door barred, every window closed off.

The first cry rose.

It resounded through the empire like a lion's roar, a spark that ignited every street into a blazing fire. The Persians surged with hatred, swords flashing in the sunlight and spittle flying from their lips. They charged into Jewish homes with great shouts. Where a people would have accepted their fate before now rose, emerging from doorways and alleys with a fierce glint in their eyes.

Steel clashed against steel. Dust billowed in great clouds beneath the skidding of feet and the collapsing of corpses. Smoke lifted over rooftops. It was impossible to distinguish Persian blood from Jewish blood as red streamed through the streets. The clamor and cries were unrelenting.

By nightfall, fear had changed sides. The Jews shouted in victory as they set fire to the bodies of their oppressors, once so strong, now piled in heaps on the ground.

Esther watched from behind the palace walls. She pressed her hand against the window, her heart ablaze with the pulsating fires of her people. Deliverance had arrived. She stepped out onto the balcony, overlooking the city and the clouds of smoke rising from burning skin. The smell of ash and flesh filled her senses, and the heat cast a warm glow over her skin.

She recognized the steady rhythm of King Xerxes's footsteps as he approached her from behind. "Queen Esther, my guards have alerted me that Haman's sons all perished in the battle."

"What of his wife?"

"Dead. Found by the river with a knife in her chest."

Esther's heart swirled with a grim satisfaction. "Was each body recovered?"

A nod.

"Hang them all," said Esther. "Hang them on gallows beside Haman. Evil must be put to rest." A spirit of vengeance roused within her, a spirit that took up its sword and demanded redemption. "Allow the Jews to seize justice tomorrow, as well. They may do what they have done today once again."

"As you wish, Queen Esther."

———

Two weeks. That was all it had taken to make the once-mighty Supreme Chief of Persia utterly unrecognizable.

The foulest stench hung in the air, the stench of rotting wickedness. His head hung at a disturbingly unnatural angle. The coarse rope at his neck had blackened with blood. Flies buzzed around the sickly green skin, parts of flesh and teeth scattered across the dirt below. Haman the Agagite had wasted away. Only the maggots remained to feast upon his organs.

But he was no longer alone. His family swung beside him, eyes shut and bodies paling by the hour. The once voluptuous dunes of Zeresh's body now sagged in a grotesque stillness. The once intimidating cuts of his sons' shoulders hung limply, dark silhouettes against the bright day.

The world continued turning as nature slowly enacted one final act of justice.

30

**ER FATHER WAS DEAD.** Found mutilated in the city square with a spear sticking from his chest. Kyra had not seen the body. She didn't want to.

"You killed him," her mother had spat. "You should never have come here—you told him to fight. Why couldn't you have remained in the king's bed where you belong?"

"I told him to fight with the Jews," Kyra cried, her chest tightening with anguish. "I told him he would die trying to kill the Israelites, but he didn't listen. You cannot blame me."

"Get out," her mother shrieked. "You tell us to side with the Jews, and then you kill my husband. Go back to your perfumes and silks. It's the only thing you're good for."

But Kyra never returned to the harem. After the victory of the Jews, Queen Esther had stepped into the House of

Women once again, this time with a parchment sealed by the king's ring. *You are free,* she said. Kyra remembered the fierce steadiness of her gaze, the careful deliberation with which she spoke.

Freedom was glorious, but it had left her with nowhere to go. Kyra stood outside the entrance of the throne room, marveling at the opulence of the space. The cool marble seeped through the soles of sandals. Sunlight spilled from the tall windows and caught in the polished floors until the whole chamber seemed to glow. Footsteps approached behind her as Hegai rounded the corner of the corridor.

"She will see you now, Kyra," he said, a softness in his voice she did not remember from the harem.

She drew a deep breath. The air tasted faintly of incense and myrrh. She had crossed this threshold only once before, on the day Esther had been crowned. She remembered the weight of her chest then, the way her hands had curled into themselves as Esther accepted the king's hand with a smile. The burden of her remorse was great, but she would never forget the resentment. The contempt of knowing Esther had never truly wanted the crown, and yet she had received it. She had never yearned for glory, but it was granted to her. Kyra had a reason to be royalty. Esther had not. But as she looked at the softness of Esther's gaze upon crossing over into the throne room, Kyra's heart ached. Esther was the queen of Persia, but she had also been her closest companion.

She looked different. There was a calm regality to her, an elegance of wisdom. Kyra bowed before the raised dais, feeling tears spring into her eyes.

"Queen Esther," she began, "I asked you for freedom, and you gave it to me. But my mother—" her throat tightened. "My mother will not receive me. I have nowhere to go."

The vastness of the room pressed inward.

"I am not worthy to ask more of you. But, please, if there's anything—"

Kyra stiffened in surprise as Esther enveloped her in a fierce embrace. Her arms were warm, familiar. She felt Esther's shoulders tremble in quiet tears.

"I've missed you," Esther whispered, her words breaking at the edges.

Kyra swallowed the lump in her throat. When Esther drew back, her eyes shone with something achingly unchanged.

"You're home now, Kyra."

The word settled somewhere deep in her chest, loosening a tight knot she had not known existed.

And she wept.

31

STHER GAZED AT THE BOWL OF WATER BEFORE HER, studying her reflection. She looked older. Youth had not fully escaped her, but her eyes creased with a wisdom only gifted by experience.

She splashed water into her face, dabbing the droplets before walking out onto the balcony. She removed the silken robe from her shoulders. The chill of the night whispered against her bare arms.

The moon shone brightly, beaming over Susa in a soft glow. Esther watched as candle lights flickered inside homes, shutting off one by one. The Jews would sleep safely tonight, as they would for years and years to come.

Esther craned her neck towards the heavens until only the sky's midnight canvas was in view. The stars were out tonight, twinkling more beautifully than she'd ever remembered. What had she used to say? *The stars were a map of every life, every person. Someone fearfully and wonderfully created.*

She smiled slightly to herself. She remembered looking out into the same sky through that small window in Mordecai's old house, the house of simple linen dresses and home-cooked meals and the occasional rodent. Esther thought of the girl who once believed her life could only be lived through her imagination, through fabricated stories. Her world was only as large as she deigned to make it. The crown had broadened her outlook, her heart for those around her.

Esther closed her eyes, letting moonlight and starlight blend across her skin. She was the Queen of Persia. Life was fragile, and her crown could not alter that truth. One day, she too would pass and join her ancestors. But even long after she was gone, the stars would still bear witness.

Her people had endured.

———

Esther had almost forgotten this dream paradise. She had returned behind closed eyelids, but something was different. The surrounding life had grown richer, more abundant. The greens were greener, flowers brighter, grass softer beneath her feet. Jasmine filled the air, sweet and strong, but never overpowering.

Esther braced herself for disaster, a shadow to mar the beauty—another desert illusion, a poisoned fruit, or some cruel trick of memory. She knew now that the bliss never lasted forever.

But nothing came.

Esther laughed. She laughed and laughed and danced through the lush grove, the spring greenery like a cloud beneath her feet. She fell back on the grass, surrendering to the waves of happiness coursing through her. The sun kissed her skin, and she closed her eyes, eyelashes brushing the peak of her cheekbones. Light and warmth settled over her, carrying her heart and soul into a timeless embrace.

EPILOGUE

One year later

ND THAT IS HOW QUEEN ESTHER SAVED THE JEWS OF THE PERSIAN EMPIRE."

Leila scrunched her nose. "I already know this story, *Achoti*. Why are you telling me again? Besides," Leila propped her hands on her hips, smiling proudly. "I'm friends with Queen Esther. If I didn't know her story, I could simply ask her."

Zelah laughed. She playfully caressed her sister's cheek, plump and pink with the blessing of childhood. "Leila, Her Majesty is very busy. By royal command, the Israelites are to recognize Purim every year to honor their victory. And since you wish to join Amir and Shadi so much, we must get to work."

Leila hummed, tossing vegetables in a bowl with her hands. "I suppose you're right. I'm excited about this

276

marvelous food." Leila eyed the cucumbers greedily, imagining the crunch in her mouth.

Zelah rolled her eyes, a faint smile tugging at her lips. A comfortable silence settled between them as the sisters worked side by side, arranging plates and crafting dishes in an unhurried rhythm.

"*Achoti*, what changed your mind about the Jews?"

Zelah paused, disarmed by the sudden inquiry. "Well, I suppose *you* changed my mind, Leila. And Queen Esther."

"I did?" Leila's eyes went wide with disbelief. "I had thought nothing could change your mind."

"Queen Esther is an Israelite, and she saved your life," Zelah replied as she washed vegetables in a water basin. "That was what changed my mind. And now I'm helping you make a Purim feast for you and your friends to enjoy tonight."

"Why do they call it that, anyway?"

"Call it what?"

"Purim." Leila scrunched her nose. "It sounds funny off my tongue."

"Well," Zelah began, adopting the patient tone she often reserved for her younger sister. "It's named after what Haman used to choose the time of the Jews' death, but we know Queen Esther and the great Mordecai transformed this evil into something good. Now stop scrunching your nose—you're going to get wrinkles."

"Then why not name it after Queen Esther? Or Mordecai? Why name it after the bad man?"

Zelah laughed. "That is a question you will need to ask the queen yourself. Now close your mouth and start chopping more. We must make enough for all of your friends, and you've barely cut enough for your greedy little stomach."

"Hey!" Leila shoved her sister.

The sisters' strings of laughter blended with the merriment of the empire as cities filled with feasts and music. Candles flickered on every table, the scent of fresh bread and ripe fruit mingling with the rhythm of drums and the hum of joyous voices.

Esther and Mordecai stepped from the palace into the streets, greeted by kisses on their hands and bows at their feet. Soon they returned to the palace, where a lavish Purim celebration awaited, honeyed pastries and sun-ripened fruits glistening against the mahogany table. Mordecai took his place at the king's right hand.

Xerxes thrust his wine goblet into the air. "To Mordecai the Great."

Esther mirrored the gesture. "To my Abba." Their glasses met in melodic clinks.

She smiled.

ACKNOWLEDGEMENTS

Writing is both demanding and deeply rewarding. This novel would not exist without the support of so many incredible people.

To my parents, my number one supporters in life. Thank you for your wisdom and for pouring so much love into your occasionally emotional and burnt-out-from-school daughter.

To Isaiah, who always accepts whatever insults I throw at him. Contrary to what I say, you're a pretty great older brother. I hope you didn't just skim this book.

To 이모 and the Oh Clan—my favorite Korean Texans—thank you for your endless encouragement.

To Elise, thank you for your infinite wisdom and joy. You have been such a light in my life.

To Audrey Hahn, the sister I never had. Your counsel has grown my faith more than you know.

To Ms. Shapiro, thank you for your constant encouragement and for helping me grow as a writer. Your kindness has meant more than I can say.

To Uncle Paul Kang, my very first supporter when I began this story in middle school. I can't wait to see you again.

To my LWC family, you guys are my home. Thank you for the love you've shown me all these years.

To my Father in Heaven, thank You for Your infinite grace. You've humbled me greatly, and You've loved me greatly. This is Your story, not mine.

And to you, dear reader, thank you for stepping into this story. Never believe the lie that your life is insignificant.

ABIGAIL HOPE KIM is a young writer with a passion for all things creative. Fueled by chamomile tea and a love for storytelling, writing is the one thing keeping her sane in high school. You can visit her website at itsabigailhopekim.com or find her on Instagram and TikTok at @itsabigailhopekim.